THE MATRIMONY

THE KNOT
BOOK 2

D. ROSE

Copyright © 2023 by D. Rose

All rights reserved.

No part of this book may be reproduced in any form or by any electronic or mechanical means, including information storage and retrieval systems, without written permission from the author, except for the use of brief quotations in a book review.

BEFORE YOU START THE MATRIMONY

For the best reading experience, it is recommended that The Vow be read before The Matrimony.

Happy Reading.

CONTENTS

Chapter 1	1
Chapter 2	11
Chapter 3	25
Chapter 4	39
Chapter 5	53
Chapter 6	65
Chapter 7	81
Chapter 8	91
The end	99
XO	101
Acknowledgments	103
Also by D. Rose	105

THE MATRIMONY

Love is the easiest thing in the world when it happens by accident, but it doesn't get real until you do it on purpose.

-ELLIE FROM **ENTERGALACTIC**

CHAPTER ONE

Sergio

"WHEN ARE YOU COMING TO BED?"

I looked up from my monitor and met Michaela's tired eyes. She tilted her head to the side with a raised eyebrow. My gaze traveled over Michaela, taking in every inch of her, from the black scarf covering her shoulder length hair to the pink silk robe adorning her frame, which was my favorite. I bought it while in Italy this past summer.

After wrapping my latest movie, we spent the week there reconnecting. That trip seemed so long ago, and we hadn't taken one since then. With my film in post-production, editing and promotion had stolen every free minute I had. When I got home this evening, she wasn't here, so I ordered takeout and kept myself busy with edits.

"Sergio," she called out, snapping me out of my thoughts.

Licking my bottom lip, I returned my attention to the monitor, noting the timestamp. There were a little over 30 minutes left in the film. I had extensive notes to review before sending them to Tia. The final version of my film was due in a month. There were several issues I found with audio, color, and transitions. It seemed like we'd never reach the finish line.

"Soon, baby."

She folded her arms over her chest. "Soon?"

"30 minutes," I said with a smile. She didn't smile back, instead she rolled her eyes and turned to leave. "Mick, wait. Come here."

"What is it?" She didn't bother leaving the doorway.

"Come and see."

Slowly, she walked over to me. Apprehension covered her features as I reached out for her to sit on my lap. Once settled, I wrapped my arms around her waist. I ran my nose along her neck and shoulder and inhaled. She smelled like a mixture of shea butter and coconut. Her scent had always brought me comfort. My hold tightened, prompting her to release a soft sigh.

"Where were you tonight?" I asked, still nuzzling her. It had been weeks since I held my wife. Between me traveling and her working as a brand ambassador and influencer, we hardly saw each other these days.

"I had a dinner meeting with Green Thumb Magazine.

They want to feature my line of products in their spring issue. I'll have a three-page spread and an interview."

"That's major, baby." I looked at her, noting the small smile on her lips. "We need to celebrate."

"After dinner, I went out with Kamryn and Tia for a drink." My chest tightened when her eyes narrowed at me.

"Why didn't you call me?"

She shrugged. "I wasn't sure if you would make it. Besides, Tia had already told us about how stressful edits had been for you. So, I figured you'd be here, doing this."

Michaela motioned her hands at the monitors in front of us. I nodded as heat flooded my cheeks and knots twisted in my stomach. Silence fell over us and I resumed playing the movie. Michaela remained on my left thigh, moving only when I reached for my tablet to take notes.

"Tia says your notes aren't due for another two weeks."

"Yeah, but I'm going to New York on Wednesday. I have a meeting with Reed Hudlin about directing a drama series. He's been all over the place, and I don't want him affecting the timeline for '*Burden of Truth*.' I want to have my notes done before I leave."

Michaela hummed. "And after New York, you're heading to Dallas, right?"

I nodded. "Yeah, I'm presenting at the Black Film Awards."

"Another month of barely seeing each other," she mused.

"Mick, come on." I paused the movie while pushing out a sigh. "I know it is busy, but the holidays are around the corner."

"And when the new year comes, you'll be traveling again, and it'll be award season. I know, Serg." Her mouth twisted. I could tell she was holding back, and that shit made my ears hot.

"Are you not coming with me to the Golden Globes and Oscars awards?"

My forehead wrinkled at the incredulity in her tone. Walking the red carpet together had been our dream since *Mama and Me* premiered two years ago.

"Of course I am. It's just... never mind. I'm going to bed." She attempted to leave my lap, but I held her in place.

"Talk to me, Mick."

Her coffee-colored eyes darkened, and her nostrils flared. We hardly talked anymore. Our text messages were quick updates, and phone calls were few. When I was home, Michaela would work at The Plant Shop or in her greenhouse in the backyard. I wasn't sure how we got here. Or why we let it get this bad, but I needed for us to get back on track.

"What is it you need from me?"

Michaela sighed. "I'm tired and I don't want to fight with you."

"We're not fighting, baby."

I kissed her neck, pleased with the soft moan that slipped from her lips. After dropping a few more kisses on her shoulder, she relaxed in my arms. I could sense her guard lowering. She used to be so open and honest with me. I didn't have to force her to share her feelings and thoughts. It was harder for me to gauge her these days. Her eyes were unreadable, and her tone stayed level, even when we were disagreeing. I hated it. There was nothing I disliked more than seeing my wife unhappy. Whatever I needed to do to smooth things over, I would do it. I just needed her to tell me what she wanted from me.

"I miss you," she confessed moments later. "You're hardly home anymore. And when you are home, you're here working."

I untied her robe and slipped my hands in between her thighs. A smile covered my face when I learned she wasn't wearing anything underneath. She opened her legs for me, her heated gaze never wavering from mine.

"I miss you too." I groaned at the feel of her wetness. "I know I haven't been the best husband lately. Mick, I will make it up to you. I promise."

"Talk is cheap."

My mouth slouched as I nodded. It would take more than talking to fix this. "True. Will you give me a chance to make it up to you?"

She shrugged. "Depends. How much longer until you come to bed?"

I repositioned her on my lap so that she was sitting in the middle. Using my thumb, I ran slow circles around her clit while kissing and nipping her neck. She held onto the arms of my chair and laid her head on my shoulder. Her moans were soft and filled with desire. My other hand traversed her frame from her stomach to her taut nipples. I gently tweaked and tugged her nipples, pulling another moan from her.

Damn, it had been so long since I felt her and held her this close. In the beginning, we couldn't keep our hands off each other. I refused to believe it was because we were newlyweds. I didn't believe in the "honeymoon" stage because what we had was deeper than a phase. Our arrangement wasn't ideal, but it worked out in our favor. I had fallen in love with Michaela and couldn't imagine my life without her.

"Serg, I need to feel you," she breathed.

I kissed the curve of her neck. She didn't know how desperately I needed to feel her. Just a few days ago, Tia made a remark about how tense I'd been lately. I could only attribute the stress to upcoming deadlines and constant traveling. Never would I admit it was because I had been neglecting my wife at home. Not only was it no one's business, I was ashamed of becoming such a shit husband. I forgot the blessing I had at home because I was so focused on work.

I lifted Michaela from my lap and turned her to face me. Unmitigated desire and longing danced in her eyes. My dick throbbed at the mere sight of her. I cupped her cheek, taking in her radiant mocha colored skin, coffee brown eyes, round nose, and soft full-shaped lips. She held onto the edge of my desk as I pulled down my joggers and underwear. I hooked my arm around her waist to hoist her onto the desk. She shuddered a breath when my dick poked at her opening. Michaela's head fell back as I inched into her. I hissed at her warmth and tightness.

"I'm sorry, baby," I said, staring deeply into her eyes. She bit her bottom lip and looked away. That shit hit me right in the chest. Even during sex, she remained distant. I rocked into her, my cadence slow and sensual as I slipped her robe from her shoulder. "Look at me."

When she didn't, I cupped her cheek, bringing her attention back to me.

"How can I fix it?"

She shook her head; tears pooling in her eyes. "Not now," she breathed. "I don't want to talk."

Shit.

Before any tears could fall, she closed her eyes. Her arms circled my neck and one leg dangled from my waist. I hooked the other over my arm and dove deeper into her.

I kissed her slowly, savoring the taste of her lips and tongue. She kissed me back with just as much vigor. Her pecks communicating all the things she didn't want to say. If only she knew how badly I missed her. The feeling wasn't one-sided by any means. As much as I loved my career, I loved lunging around all-day with her, going on dates, and taking trips. Sadly, the last time we did any of those things was this summer.

"I love you," I told her when she ended our kiss. "So, fucking much."

She gripped the edge of my desk, moving her hips in a rhythm that was hard for me to keep up with, but dammit if I didn't try. Michaela pushed back my tablet and keyboard, making space for her to spread wider. My strokes were faster now, pushing Michaela to her inevitable brink. I held her tighter, my knees buckled, and my groin tightened from the wetness coating me. Her mouth met mine as she unraveled before me.

Our breaths were choppy, the rhythm frenzied as I rocked into her. Each stroke was more fervid than before. She dug her nails into my shoulder; the sharp pain was soon replaced with pleasure when she kissed me. Her tongue pressed at the seams of my lips. When I met her tongue with mine, she pushed out a guttural moan.

"I love you too, Serg," she whimpered. The softness in her tone pulled at my heart. Her eyes were so low, yet I could see the yearning glimmering in them. I let out a deep, rumbling groan and thrusted into her one last time. Her body went limp in my arms. I planted my hand on the desk, securing her against me.

"Mick, I-"

"Come to bed," she said against my lips. I reared back, meeting her intense gaze. There was no room for compromise tonight. She needed me.

With a nod, I replied, "Your wish is my command."

The following morning, I woke up to my alarm and the sun peeking through the blinds. I snatched my phone from the nightstand. I turned over, expecting to see Michaela glaring at me. She hated the sound of my alarm. Most mornings, she woke up before me to hit snooze. After turning it off, I scrolled through my notifications. Missed calls, meeting reminders, text messages, and I didn't even bother checking my socials.

I sat up and brushed my hand over my face.

Where the hell was Michaela?

Just as I was about to call her, Tia's name appeared on my screen.

"Hey, T."

"Rise and shine! You have four meetings today. Are we going to the office?"

"Nah. I'm not in the mood for LA traffic. Besides, all the meetings are virtual, correct?"

"Mhm. I'll grab breakfast and be there in an hour."

I nodded. "Sounds good. Hey, have you heard from Mick today?"

Tia was quiet for a beat. "Yeah. She's at breakfast with Kamryn."

"They always go to breakfast?"

"A few times a week," she hummed. "You can call her, you know?"

"Okay. Cool. I'll call her in a few." I tried for a quick recovery, but it was pointless. The awkward tension that occurred whenever I brought up Michaela couldn't be ignored.

"Cool," she chirped. "Oh, Mecca sent a script last night."

My eyebrow rose. "Mecca? He was serious?"

This past March, Mecca and I went to dinner and talked about a script he'd been writing. I was used to people telling their ideas and never following through. Mecca wanted to write a movie loosely based on his life. The coming-of-age tale followed three young men as they maneuvered life in Houston. He wanted to focus on how he and his manager, Puma, navigated the loss of their childhood friend, Victor.

I was especially interested in learning more about that period of his life. Mecca hadn't ever talked about the passing of Victor until recently, when Victor's younger sister, Heaven, signed to the same label as the mogul-rapper.

"He's so serious. And the script is good. I read it in under two hours."

"I guess I need to read it then."

"Yup. Text me what you want for breakfast."

"Got you. Can you call Chef Greg and see if he's available tonight?"

"Tonight?" she shrieked. "You know he prefers bookings in advance."

I sighed. "I know, I know, but this is... an emergency."

Tia belted out a laugh. "Operation: Get Your House in Order has begun, huh? Let me send an SOS text."

"What's that supposed to mean, T?" I tilted my head to the side with pinched eyebrows. My chest tightened at the thought of her knowing something I didn't. Different scenarios ran through my mind, making my jaw clench and nostrils flare. "Mick said something?"

"No, not really. I'm the one in charge of your schedule. There have been more dinner meetings and fewer dates on the calendar lately. Any who, Greg replied to my text saying he's available. He will be at your house by four and will email you a menu in an hour. Anything else?"

Running my hand over my head, I sighed. "Yeah, get me a few quotes for a cabin in Beaver Creek."

I heard the smile in her tone when she replied, "I'll get right to it."

CHAPTER TWO

Michaela

MY MOUTH WATERED when our waitress placed a big icing covered cinnamon roll onto our table. Kamryn's eyes widened and her hand went to her belly. Her light brown skin was radiant these days. Soft, tight coils framed her face. A broad smile covered her features as she eyed the dessert.

"This baby has impeccable taste." She picked up her fork and stabbed the soft pastry. "I crave these at least twice a week."

I used my fork and knife to cut a piece. "I know. You

guys are the reason I couldn't button my jeans this morning."

Kamryn laughed. "Don't blame us. You're the one who stopped going to Pilates."

"Because my gym buddy changed her workout routine."

"Hubs wants me to take it easy. So, yoga twice a week and daily walks are all I can do. Sorry." She faked a pout. "Besides, the shop keeps me active enough."

Since becoming The Plant Shop's brand ambassador, business had been on a steady climb. My YouTube channel and social media presence landed me a partnership with Green's Love, a holistic gardening company. We are in the middle of creating a line of potting mix and gardening tools. The items would be sold only at The Plant Shop and on Green Love's website.

Green's Love marketing team had us on a strict rollout that called for late nights and several meetings a week. They wanted Kamryn and me to be a part of every aspect of the rollout. From deciding who gets PR packages to the guest list for the launch party; our opinions mattered. The added pressures of scaling a business forced her to make several lifestyle changes. She worked shorter hours, hired more staff, and started a less strenuous workout routine.

"Well, I guess I'll have to find another partner." I waved my fork while rolling my eyes.

"I won't hold it against you."

We were silent for a beat as we indulged in the pastry before us. Twice a week before work, we stopped by the Corner Cafe for breakfast. This had become our routine after I returned to work. Toward the end of my master's program, I had to quit The Plant Shop to lighten my load. Becoming an influencer had opened the windows of opportunity for me. I used my status to help Kamryn. After all, it was the least I could do since she'd taken me under her wing all those years ago.

These days, The Plant Shop was so busy that we hardly had time to chat about personal matters. By the end of our shifts, we were too beat to talk about anything. Sometimes, Kamryn would lend her ear after work and listen to me lament about how much I missed Sergio. Other times, she'd encourage me to tell him how I felt; I rarely heeded to that advice.

"So, have you talked to your husband?" Kamryn's eyes narrowed at me. I shook my head while continuing to chew. "Michaela," she droned.

After washing down my bite with water, I replied, "We didn't really have time to talk."

I knew how badly we needed to talk, but when I saw him at his desk working so diligently, I reconsidered.

Kamryn's smirk pulled a shriek of laughter from me. "That is an excellent way to break the tension."

"I wouldn't say there's tension." I paused, searching for the right words to describe the shift between us. "More like awkward energy or something. I don't know what to call it; I'm just ready to get over this hump."

"The only way to do that is by talking to him," she chirped.

"Kam," I whined. "He's so busy juggling multiple projects, getting pulled in a million different directions, and his career is finally where he wants it to be. I'd never forgive myself for making him feel guilty about it."

She shook her head. "No, no. You're not making him choose between you and his career. You're simply asking for him to make time for you, and y'all's marriage. What y'all are going through is nothing new. Couples experience the "terrible twos" phase in one way or another."

"Not this again," I groused.

Terrible Twos.

Thanks to Kamryn, I had become familiar with the term. I rolled my eyes, remembering the blogs I'd read a few weeks back. During a restless night of missing Sergio, I browsed marriage blogs and read about the terrible twos. Most blogs cited major life changes as a cause, and it made me think about our union.

"I'm serious. Hubs and I went through our rough patch, too. We were working on the business plan for The Plant Shop, and he had landed his first job after obtaining his Ph.D. Sometimes we get so caught in the grind, we forget to nurture the relationships most important to us."

"All that happened in two years?"

"More like three-and-a-half, but still. It happened."

"How did you all get through it?" I pressed.

There weren't many people I could go to for advice. My uncle and his wife, Denice, were too overprotective. And not just over me, but with Sergio, too. Kamryn was my safe space.

She smirked. "By addressing the problem, and then attempting to change things. You and Sergio are still new. Everything happened kind of fast and while I believe in love at first sight; it takes time to establish a rhythm. You're not a graduate student working several jobs and an internship anymore. Sergio's career catapulted into another realm after *Mama and Me* with no signs of slowing down."

I hummed while cutting another piece of our cinnamon roll.

Two years ago, Sergio needed me to clean his image after his sex-tape leaked. In turn, he helped me financially. We'd fallen in love in the midst of it all, and sometimes I worried Sergio had lost sight of us. Our arrangement was still our best kept secret, and after listening to Kamryn, I realized we were still a *new* couple.

I wasn't sure what Sergio was thinking. Communication between us was at its worst, and the longer it went on, the harder it became to open up. With him constantly on the go, I didn't want to ruin his time home with an argument.

"How do we feel about Amber?" Kamryn's question halted my thoughts.

"She's cool, I guess. She doesn't email me after hours, unlike her VPs, so she's good in my book."

Kamryn covered her mouth, stifling her giggles. "I don't know if I like her."

"What? Why?"

"She *never* smiles and is so uptight. I asked about her weekend, she ignored me. It's all about the business with her."

"And that's a bad thing?"

She rolled her eyes. "Did you notice she sent a mockup of your display within 48 hours? I still don't know how she did it. We aren't launching until the summer, and she already wants to start building the display. We haven't even completed the new layout for the shop."

"Kam, relax. She wants to see where we want it. There may be a better location that fits her vision. Oh, did you see her invite? She wants to introduce us to the company that's building the display. Are we okay with meeting at 9:30 tomorrow?"

"We don't open until ten," Kamryn replied curtly.

Office hours didn't exist in this industry. It was expected to be available at any moment. Emails and text messages came at all hours of the day and night. As much as I hated their lack of respect for boundaries, I realized the importance of my partnership with Green's Love. I was willing to make temporary sacrifices to advance my career. Kamryn, however, didn't share the same sentiment.

"Okay. I'll tell her ten is better," I said to Kamryn with a smile.

"Great." Kamryn's strained smile made me sputter out a laugh.

Ten minutes later we were walking to The Plant Shop as I carried Kamryn's cinnamon roll in my hand. I looped my other arm around hers as we discussed paint colors for the nursery. Kamryn leaned in, showing me the garden-themed nurseries she'd seen on Pinterest. The air was cool, but the sun shined bright as we rounded the corner to our street.

Our strides slowed when we found a guy lingering at the front door. His delivery truck was parked at the curb with the hazard lights on. In his arms was a massive bouquet of red roses. He tapped his foot on the pavement while scrolling through his phone.

When he caught my gaze, he nodded. "Hey, I got a delivery for Michaela Jones."

"That'll be her," Kamryn interjected while nudging my side. While she disengaged the alarm from her phone, I accepted my flowers and note card. After signing the confirmation form, Kamryn and I headed inside.

"What does it say?" She was practically on my heels as I walked to the register.

"I haven't been to Michaela's Haven in a minute. Meet me there at seven." I tried my best to act unaffected. Luckily, she couldn't see the butterflies swarming my belly or the warmth flooding my cheeks.

"Ooh. What's Michaela's Haven?" Kamryn shimmied her shoulders.

"My greenhouse," I said with an eye roll. "We used to have dinners in the backyard near it. Depending on the season, I'd have flowers and vines cascading into the greenhouse. After dinner, we'd have a nightcap at the firepit." I sighed after recalling the time we fell asleep on the lounge chair after one too many glasses of wine.

"Sounds like the perfect time to tell him how you've been feeling."

I twirled the card between my thumb and index finger. "And risk ruining a romantic dinner?"

"Fine. Don't listen to the woman who's been married for nearly a decade." Kamryn snickered. After a three-second stare down, I folded.

"Okay. I'll do it."

"Good. You'll feel much better afterward."

"I hope you're right."

I picked up the card and read the message once more. Anxiety had replaced the butterflies from earlier. Gestures like these couldn't be appreciated fully as long as I held my tongue. The longer I mulled over Kamryn's advice, the more I realized I didn't have a choice but to talk to him.

AT PRECISELY SEVEN on the dot, I walked into our home. Tucked under my arm was the bouquet Sergio had delivered to my job this morning. I placed the arrangement on the bench while slipping off my shoes. The sound of footsteps caught my attention, prompting me to look at the end of the entryway.

"Hey, baby," he crooned with a smirk.

Dressed in a sage colored linen set, Sergio looked deliciously handsome. The color complimented his caramel-colored skin. The top three buttons of his shirt were opened, exposing his gold herringbone chain. He tucked one hand in his pocket while holding a glass of wine in my direction.

I walked over to him, happily accepting the chilled glass of chardonnay wine. His fiery, sienna-colored eyes remained on me as I took my first sip.

"How was your day?"

"It was busy. But I had something to look forward to after leaving, so that made it better. Thanks for the flowers."

Sergio grabbed me by the waist, pulled me flush against him. He kissed my forehead before saying, "There's a vase waiting for them near the window."

I nodded. "Do I have time to trim my roses?"

He shook his head. "Chef is plating our appetizer as we speak."

"Okay. Well, can you put them in water while I change?"

"Of course," he said before dropping a peck onto my lips.

I hurried upstairs to change into something more appropriate for a candlelight dinner. The t-shirt and baggy jeans I wore to work wouldn't suffice. After slipping into a black dress, I brushed my hair, grateful for the fresh silk press I got two days ago. Minutes later, I was back downstairs, sipping my wine as I strode through the kitchen.

Chef Greg and his assistants were hard at work preparing our dinner.

"Evening, Chefs." Everyone looked up and greeted me with smiles.

"Mrs. Jones. It's good to see you again."

"Likewise. What's on the menu tonight?" I leaned onto the kitchen island, eager to hear what he cooked for us.

Chef Greg clapped his hands together. "Lobster bisque soup to start, then Chilean sea bass with rice pilaf and a vegetable medley. For dessert, key lime pie."

"Everything sounds delicious," I mused. Chef Greg smiled before going back to cutting vegetables. I continued to the backyard; butterflies danced in my belly when I found Sergio seated in front of the fire pit. He was on his phone, predictably, while drinking a glass of wine. There was a small table for two near the seating area, surrounded by tea lights.

"You like it?" he asked, while locking his phone and putting it away. He strode over to me with an unreadable expression.

With a nod, I replied, "I love it."

I sensed his relief when he replied, "Good."

He pulled out my chair, then waited for me to sit. A wave of heat covered me when he grazed my shoulder after pushing my chair to the table. I took a gulp of my wine. Everything was perfect, from hiring Chef Greg to cook for us to having dinner near my greenhouse. Did I want to ruin the vibe by bringing the weirdness I was feeling?

"How was work?" Sergio's question interrupted my thoughts.

After another sip of wine, I replied, "Amber from Green's Love came by to discuss my potting soil display. She wants it in the windows and Kam wants it next to our gardening supplies. I get both, but I'm leaning more toward Amber's idea, since this is her area of expertise."

"You haven't told Kam, huh?"

I shook my head. "By the time Amber left, she wasn't in the mood to discuss the display any further. I get it because she has a business to run. My product placement is just a small drop in her pond. Online orders are thriving, and she hasn't hired a dedicated person to fulfill the orders yet."

"Where do you fit in all of this?"

"I'm still the brand ambassador and assistant manager."

"What about your own plant business?"

My forehead wrinkled. "Not interested. Working with Kamryn is as close as I'd get to running a business."

The sound of footsteps interrupted our conversation as Chef Greg, and his assistant brought out our first dish. I inhaled deeply and moaned at the aroma of his famous soup. After listening to Chef's spiel about the dish, I grabbed my spoon and dug in.

"Still your favorite?"

"Yup. That'll never change."

Humor danced in his eyes. A tightness formed in my stomach the longer he stared at me. He reached across the table for my hand. I looked down at our interlocked fingers, wondering how the hell we got here. It had been months since we sat down for a simple dinner date. Late meetings, jetlag, and poor communication ultimately led to us spending less time together. Neither of us questioned the distance. We just adapted to it. When Sergio wasn't in town, I split my time between my uncle and Kamryn. My greenhouse and growing status in the plant community kept me occupied, too.

Forcing myself to keep busy wasn't enough to stop me from missing him. In July, when he wrapped his film, *Burden of Truth*, we spent a in Italy. We spent our days aboard a yacht, catching rays and making up for lost time. When we were back on land, we dined at the finest restaurants and shopped until my heart was content. Things were moving in the right direction or so I thought. A month after returning home, Sergio was back to his regularly scheduled meetings. The hole kept getting deeper and deeper.

"What's on your mind?" he asked.

"Work stuff."

His eyebrows shot up for me to continue. "You're worried about the launch?"

"Yes. Amongst other things. Green's Love is interested

in me making a full line of products. Of course, this is contingent upon how well my potting mix does, but they're serious about expanding my brand."

"Do you miss working in the lab?"

I nodded. "I do, but I wasn't happy. When I first pursued neuroscience, it was to finish what my mother started, not because it was my passion. Working with Kamryn at her shop was my happy place. The greenhouse you all built for me only ignited my passion even more. I'm happy to be back with her and working to create my legacy."

Sergio's eyes glimmered with pride. The sight made my heart flutter and cheeks warm.

"Mick, you're making big moves. I'm proud of you." He licked his lips. "I'm sorry I couldn't make the outing last night. I hope this makes up for it." Waving his hands, he motioned at the table.

"It's a start," I teased with a grin. "But I want to talk to you about something serious."

Sergio straightened his posture, and facial expression fell flat. "It's about last night, right? I should've waited until the morning to work on edits. My plan was to stop when you got home, but I got in the zone and time got away from me. I apologize for not being attentive."

Biting my lip, I willed my heart to stop racing. "I accept your apology. But it's more than just last night. Things have been... off between us lately." He nodded slowly, assuring me the feelings weren't one-sided. "We don't really see each other. When we are together, it's like we're catching up until the next time."

He wiped his hand over his face. "I know. I feel the same way."

The sound of his phone ringing made my blood boil.

"It's T. I have to answer. She's working on something important for me."

"Go ahead," I said with a wave of my hand. Hurriedly, he left the table and answered the call. Moments later, Chef Greg brought out the main course and refilled our wineglasses. At the sound of dishes clinking, Sergio returned with the phone to his ear.

"Mick, I need five minutes. You can start eating without me."

I waved for him to go, trying my best to mask my annoyance. Tia knew how badly I needed this time with him. She remained neutral as best as she could, not really swaying either way, no matter how much I vented to her. There had to be a delicate balance between us. Not only was she his assistant, but she was also our dearest friend. And I didn't want her to feel caught in the middle.

Chef Greg and I looked at each other once Sergio left. His eyes were apologetic and his smile polite. Once the food was served, everyone went back inside, leaving me alone at the table. My jaw clenched as I looked over the perfectly plated meal before me.

I wanted to believe that this dinner was his attempt at putting us first. This evening was almost perfect. The flowers, this romantic dinner, and finally talking about the distance. We were so close to making progress. While shaking my head, I picked up my fork and started eating dinner.

CHAPTER THREE

Sergio

"T, this is the worst possible time to call," I said through gritted teeth. The disappointment in my baby's eyes when I told her to eat without me pulled at my heart. "You know how important tonight is for me."

"I know. I held off for as long as I could. The studio has been blowing *me* up. Terri was arrested for driving drunk tonight in Manhattan."

"Okay?"

"They're worried it will bring bad press to the film. The trailer drops in two weeks, and-"

"Tia, I get it. But what are we supposed to do about it?

He's a grown ass man, and they knew about his battle with addiction before casting him."

Terri Peterson, the star of *Burden of Truth*, was a nepotism baby who'd fallen off his path after his dad, Gordon Peterson, was arrested and convicted of fraud and money laundering five years ago. The only reason they hired him for the role was because his mother, Diann Peterson, was Hollywood royalty. She was the granddaughter of Harold Moore, one of the change makers in Black Hollywood. Just the mere mention of their names could get you into the right rooms. Not even the disgrace of Gordon's incarceration affected their notoriety in the industry.

"Yema was hoping you'd talk to him." The caution in Tia's tone set fire in my chest. "Listen, Sergio, I told her it wasn't a good idea, but she insisted you were the person to get through to him."

"Terri needs help, not someone preaching to him every time he fucks up. I'm the last person he needs to hear from."

I had my problems with drinking after the passing of my Big Mama. My support system saw me as more than a meal ticket. The people surrounding Terri didn't want the best for him. Not even his uncle, Deen Moore–the studio head who pushed us to cast him, cared whether he was sober. There were many days where Terri came to set too drunk to function. We had to adjust our shooting schedule to account for his late arrival and hangovers.

"You're not the preachy type."

"T," I groused. "I can't go back and forth about this

right now. Let me know when he's released. I'll find the time to talk to him after I meet with Reed. Okay?"

"Okay. I also called with good news. Everything for the trip is booked. From the flights to dinner reservations, ski lessons, shopping trips, everything. I found a service that could deliver a Christmas tree for Mick, too. They provide lights, ornaments, the whole nine."

I sighed, happy to hear the good news. "Cool. Did you talk to Kamryn about Mick's schedule? Does she have any meetings?"

"Yes. Her last meeting of the year is on the 20th. And nothing is on their calendar until the new year."

"Thanks, T. Now let's hope she's actually excited when I tell her about the trip."

Tia laughed. "I'm sure she'll love it. Now go on and break the news. I'll see you in the morning."

"Night, T."

After ending the call, I returned to Michaela. She didn't utter two words to me as I sat down at the table.

"Baby, I'm sorry about that."

"It's fine," she interjected. "Eat your food before it gets cold."

I cut into my sea bass before taking my first bite. A stifling silence settled at the dinner table. My heart raced as I thought of something to say. Michaela's eyes met mine. The ambient lighting surrounding our table danced across her soft features.

"I know we have seen little of each other lately, but I plan to fix that."

She tilted her head to the side. "And how are you going to do that?"

"By spending ten days alone in Beaver Creek." I waited for her expression to change. It didn't. There wasn't an inkling of excitement or surprise on her face. "We're going for Christmas," I continued while trying my best to sound unaffected by her silence.

"When do we leave?" she asked before sipping her wine.

"The 21st, and we'll get back on New Year's Eve in time for Mike's party."

Michaela poked her fork around her food and sighed. "Sounds good."

I sat back in my seat with furrowed eyebrows. Clearly, she wasn't thrilled about our trip, so I dropped the topic. We continued eating while making small talk in-between bites. Michaela gave me limited eye contact and one-word answers. I remained steadfast in making this a good dinner, despite being irritated by the turn of events.

An hour later we were sitting at the firepit. Michaela's feet were in my lap as she stared at the sky above. I grabbed her foot, massaging the arch with my thumb. A groan slipped from her lips. She sipped her wine, gazing at me with sultry eyes. I moved to the ball of her foot, applying more pressure than before.

"Why aren't you excited about the trip?" I asked, sensing how relaxed she'd become. She wiggled her toes, then tried to pull away from me. While shaking my head, I tugged her ankle, pulling her closer to me. My hand trailed her ankle and calf. I smirked at the goosebumps covering her skin.

"I want real change, not a trip that gets my hopes up,

like Italy. Ten days alone to reconnect just for things to go back to being like this? How can I be excited, Sergio?"

"Italy was different. That trip wasn't about us, it was work, but I still made time for us, didn't I? We'll be in the mountains alone, doing whatever you want. You'll have my undivided attention."

"Like tonight?" she asked while sitting up. "We couldn't even have dinner without work interrupting."

Michaela was on one tonight. She hadn't been this mad in a while. I licked my lip while thinking of what to say next. The last thing I wanted to say was something to set her off. After a beat, I told her the reason for the call.

"Terri was arrested for drunk driving, and the studio heads want me to talk to him."

Her expression softened as she placed her drink on the table. "Is he okay? Was anyone hurt?"

"He's fine. They'll probably release him in a few hours."

People like him didn't stay in jail long. He came from a family of wealth and power; meaning the best lawyers were always on standby.

"What are you going to say to him?"

"I don't know, baby. But I'll think of something during my flight."

She moved closer to me, placing her hand on my knee. "I know you'll say what he needs to hear to get his life on track. He's been through so much in this industry."

I nodded my head. "Yeah, he has."

There was so much Michaela didn't know about Terri's past. I prayed she never saw the dark side of Hollywood. The side that stole people's dreams and left them with nothing. I flirted with the scene a time or two, but got out before it was too late.

"I never told anyone this, but Terri and I talked about his drinking."

"What did you tell him?"

Pushing out a breath, I replied, "I told him how my partying phase started, we reminisced about the times we bumped into each other at parties and mourned the friends we lost. I just wanted him to know there was no judgment from me. We try to escape our demons the best ways we can. But I also let him know he was talented as hell, and he's needed in this industry."

Michaela smiled, exposing those dimples I adored so much. "Serg, that was really sweet of you. Next time you see him, reiterate those kind words. Maybe encourage rehab and therapy. It sounds like Terri needs an actual friend."

"Maybe he does."

Terri was born to an award-winning actress and politician. Acting was in his DNA. We liked to attribute his rich bloodline to his success, but in reality, the guy was talented. Before breaking onto the scene, he took his time honing his craft by attending Geffen School of Drama at Yale University. Terri worked with the best acting coaches and didn't rush to do anything until he was ready.

He starred in his first film just six years ago at twenty-five. Shortly after his debut, his father's scandal came to light, and that's when he took a turn. I was sure his family wrote off his alcohol abuse as a phase. For years, they'd covered up his arrests and silenced any blogs that exposed his addiction. Instead of getting him proper help, they enabled his toxic behaviors.

"You know what I realized today?" The sound of Michaela's voice broke my train of thought.

"What?" My eyebrow hiked.

"We're still a new couple."

I nodded. "I mean, yeah. It's only been two years."

"I'm not talking about just our marriage. Our entire relationship. We went on two dates before we got married."

"What are you saying, baby?"

She lifted a shoulder. Wonder glimmered in her eyes as she said, "I think we should spend more time in the courting phase. Getting to know each other on a deeper level. We're so caught up in our careers that we've neglected each other. I wasn't too thrilled when you told me about the trip because I felt it was just a temporary solution."

"It's not temporary." I shook my head vehemently. "The best way for me to connect with you is without the distractions of work and everyday life here."

"Yeah, but we need to establish a rhythm *with* our work and social life."

My forehead wrinkled. "You're right. Let's work on that tonight," I said, cupping her cheek. She smiled softly, then bit her lip. "And in the morning, maybe we can get breakfast."

Michaela simpered at me. "Since when did you become a breakfast person?"

"Since I woke up alone this morning. Why didn't you

say anything before leaving? I'd been gone for weeks. I didn't expect you to be gone in the morning."

Her eyes lowered as she gnawed on her bottom lip. I angled her chin back, making her meet my gaze.

"I'm sorry, baby," she told me after a moment. "I didn't think about it like that."

Closing the space between us, I kissed her on the lips. She straddled my lap. My hands went to her ass, pressing our bodies together.

"We haven't had sex out here in a long time," she purred in my ear while moving her hips on me.

I smiled before kissing her neck. The smell of her perfume filled my nose, sending a wave of warmth over me.

"It's been at least three months," she continued while meeting my gaze. Peering at me through heavy lids; Michaela's gaze was searing.

"We should fix that ASAP," I said, palming her ass.

She smirked. "Yeah, we should."

The soft kiss she planted on my lips sealed the deal.

I CHECKED the time on my watch, then blew out a breath. Reed was never on time for meetings, not even the ones he scheduled. I'd arrived fifteen minutes early to beat traffic in the city. Upon my arrival, Reed's assistant, Lauren, gave me a quick tour of the new office, then showed me to the waiting area.

Reed's office had a different vibe than mine. The floor to ceiling windows showcased the Brooklyn bridge a few miles in the distance. It was a dreary day in the city. The sky was overcast, and rain was predicted for later today. The office was small, with cubicles in the center and the execs had offices on each corner. Clean white walls, gray carpet, and cookie-cutter office equipment. It was more sterile and professional here. Movie posters and pictures of the team lined the walls of the waiting area. This was the only area with any personality.

To keep myself busy, I read over Mecca's script on my tablet. Tia sent her notes, and I agreed with most of them. If Mecca was serious about making a film, I'd be open to rewriting the script with him. The story had potential.

I caught Lauren's gaze from across the room, and she smiled politely.

"How much longer?" I asked her.

"I'd say ten minutes. He's finishing up a phone call."

I nodded. "Cool."

I went back to reading the script, stopping to add notes and suggestions along the way. Before I got too invested in the story, I marked the page and closed the file. There was nothing I hated more than being interrupted while reading. I pulled out my phone, intending to text Tia, but I opened Michaela's thread.

We used to text all day, every day. She'd send me selfies when I was away, giving me something to look forward to during the long days on set. I scrolled through our thread, my forehead wrinkled when I realized it had been a while since I got a picture from her. Michaela used to surprise me with lunch at the office or have something delivered when our schedules didn't align. The more I read over our messages, the more I noticed the distance growing between us.

What used to be long exchanges were now one-word responses, with several hours between messages. That needed to change. I snapped a few pictures of the view and sent them to Michaela. Seconds later she replied with heart eyes.

SERGIO:
I miss you

MICHAELA:
I miss you more. How's Reed?

SERGIO:
I wouldn't know. I'm still waiting to see him.

Michaela sent the sad face emoji that made me chuckle. I looked at the time we were almost at the fifteen-minute mark. Lauren held up her finger before disappearing into Reed's office. Another text from Michaela pinged, stealing my attention.

MICHAELA:
I saw Terri was released last night...

I pushed out a breath.

SERGIO:
He isn't taking calls. I reached out to him and his assistant.

MICHAELA:
He probably needs time.

> SERGIO:
> True. How are things on your end?

> MICHAELA:
> Great! We just got a shipment of fiddle leaf plants. We're potting them for the product shoots.

Attached was a picture of her holding one. I smiled at the sight of my wife. Her hair was in a bun, dimples were on full display, and eyes glimmered with joy. Since going back to The Plant Shop, she had a glow about her. After getting her master's degree, she decided not to pursue a Ph.D., and gave her job a two-week's notice. She spent six months traveling with me and learning more about the industry. The timing was perfect because I was on the road promoting Tia's debut film *Out of Luck*. The film didn't do as well as we hoped, but I was still proud of Tia for taking a leap of faith.

"Reed will see you now," Lauren said from across the room.

"About time."

I typed out my last message to Michaela.

> SERGIO:
> Heading into a meeting. I'll call you after.

> MICHAELA:
> Can't wait to hear all about it.

I bit back a smile while putting my phone into my pocket. Once I was inside Reed's office, I took a seat in the chair in front of his desk.

"Sorry about that, man," he said while typing away on his phone. "Jesse keeps changing the script, adding locations, and the cast keeps growing. I needed to reel him in. We begin table reads in a month."

I shook my head. Jesse Isaacs, the head writer on the show, was overzealous at times. This was his second show and undoubtedly he was feeling the pressure. Why else would he rewrite a perfect script? With Reed as his showrunner, he was in excellent hands. The entire team, from producers to me, the director, had years of experience. There was no way this show would flop.

"Jesse needs to chill. Is he the reason you've been all over the place with this show?"

Reed looked up from his computer, his expression solemn. "Exactly. We've been developing this show for three years. It's the closest to perfect as perfect can be. Things will happen, but that's the business."

I nodded, thinking about Terri's recent arrest. The studio execs called me the following morning to discuss strategy regarding the movie's rollout. I wanted to wait and see how everything panned out. If we jumped too soon, our actions could cause more harm than good. The way the media moved these days, Terri's arrest would be old news by tomorrow.

"But I'm sure you know about that already." Reed removed his glasses and placed them on the desk. "I heard about Terri."

I sighed. "Yeah. I was hoping to meet with him while in town, but he isn't answering calls."

"I don't blame him."

"Neither do I, but when Yema asks you to do something..."

"You better do it." Reed chuckled. "How's the wife?"

I couldn't help my smile when I replied, "She's good. Working on a partnership with a gardening company."

"You know, Morgan already told me. She's kept a close eye on Michaela since meeting her last year. I'm happy to see y'all are still going strong."

"Me too," I replied with a smile.

We weren't at our best, but I had faith we could get back on track. Consistency and intimacy would revive the spark between us in no time. The dinner I surprised her with was a good start. The following morning, we went to breakfast, and she told me more about her partnership with Green's Love. Her product shoot was at the top of the year along with a promo tour in major cities across the U.S. I was happy to see she was blazing her own path.

Reed clapped his hands together, snapping me from my thoughts. "Ready to start the meeting?" he asked while sifting through a stack of papers. "Lauren has everyone on the line."

I met his humorous expression and smirked. "I've been waiting for you."

CHAPTER FOUR

Michaela

I TWIRLED IN THE MIRROR, stopping to see if I liked the plunging back of the red dress I purchased for dinner. Rosé Marie poured from my Bluetooth speaker as I looked over my appearance. A smile curved my lips.

Sergio was going to lose it when he saw me. The midi form fitting dress was the perfect welcome home gift to my husband. I made reservations at our favorite restaurant for dinner, got my hair and nails done, and even bought him a gift just because. I was determined to make tonight special. He was gone for a week-and-a-half, but it felt like forever.

Since talking to Sergio, he'd been attempting to be present. He texted more and sent flowers to my job twice while he was gone. Sergio was reminding me why I fell for him. His attentiveness and support got me every time. I didn't want to jinx it, but it seemed like we were headed in the right direction.

He wasn't the only one who had things to work on in our marriage. I could admit I fell off in the romance department, too. Random lunch dates and visits to his office were things I did often at the beginning of our marriage. I couldn't pinpoint when I stopped, but I assumed it was because his schedule became too unpredictable. Or maybe I had gotten too busy with my projects to make time. Either way, I wanted to do better.

My phone rang from the bedroom, interrupting my music. I hurried from my closet to my phone that was charging on the nightstand. I was hesitant to answer when I saw it was Reyla calling via FaceTime. We never had quick conversations. With her living in San Diego, we didn't hang out as much, and our updates took at least an hour. Since our chats happened twice a month, I answered anyway. The holidays were around the corner, and I planned to be off-the-grid until the new year.

"Hey, beautiful!" she shrieked with a smile. "Where are you going looking all fine?"

Heat flooded my cheeks. "I'm going to dinner with Sergio in a few. What are you up to?"

Reyla rocked her natural loose curls that stopped at her ears. Her smile was wide, and eyes sparkled. I could tell she was genuinely happy and after the mess with Luca, she deserved it.

"Well," she droned while flashing her left hand into the camera. My eyes widened at the sight of the princess cut diamond adorning her ring finger. "Simon proposed two days ago."

"Omg, Rey! Congrats!" I jumped up and down. "Tell me everything."

I sat down in the armchair near my closet.

"We went to the Maldives to celebrate a deal he closed and on our last night, he popped the question. I haven't told anyone yet. You were the first person I wanted to share this moment with."

"Aw, Rey. I'm so happy for you. Simon is a sweetheart and seeing how happy he makes you warms my heart."

Shortly after moving to San Diego, Reyla met Simon Powell, a Chief Operating Officer at the World Trade Center. Their relationship moved fast because that was how Reyla liked it. Within six months of dating, she moved into his mansion on the water. I was surprised it took this long for them to get engaged.

"That means a lot coming from you. I was such a mess with Luca, and it almost cost me our friendship."

Her eyes glossed over with tears. I couldn't tell if she was emotional because of the engagement or if the memory of her last relationship still saddened her. Fighting back tears of my own, I cleared my throat.

"If I cry, it'll mess up my makeup," I teased.

"Please don't cry." We shared a laugh. "Anyway, we're going to have a small ceremony in Napa Valley the week of Valentine's Day. I'll send an official invitation in the coming weeks. But before that I'd love for us to have a spa day. We haven't hung out in forever."

I smiled as another wave of tears filled my eyes. Our friendship had gone through so many changes over the years. From meeting in the bathroom at a bar to becoming roommates, Reyla and I had grown up together.

"It's a date. My uncle Mike is calling. Text me the deets for our spa date. Congrats again."

"Tell your fine ass uncle I said Hey," she purred. I rolled my eyes before ending the call.

"Hey, Uncle Mike."

"Hey, Mickey. You free tonight?"

I looked down at my dress with hesitation. It was rare for me to decline an outing with my uncle. However, the plans I had for me and Sergio were more pressing at the moment.

"Denice wants to cook for you and Hollywood. We're going to Santorini for Thanksgiving this year, so she wants a family dinner before the trip."

"Nice," I replied with a smile. "I don't think Sergio can make it-"

"He's right here," Uncle Mike interjected. "Yeah, I called him after he landed earlier today and told him to stop by."

My forehead wrinkled, and my mouth twisted. "Oh. okay. What time should I come over?"

I tried to recover before my uncle could detect any signs of annoyance. The knots in my stomach tightened and my heart beat double time.

"I'll have my driver pick you up. He should be there within the hour."

I pursed my lips together and nodded. "Sounds good."

"Wait, Hollywood wants to speak to you."

"Tell him I'll see him soon."

Before my uncle could pass him the phone, I ended the call. I stormed into my closet and sifted through my clothes for something to wear. This dress was too much for a family dinner, although I considered wearing it anyway to taunt Sergio.

Just when I thought he was understanding my needs, he does this. I was too distracted to decide on an outfit, so I returned to the bedroom and checked my phone to see if I missed a call or text from him. I just couldn't believe he didn't let me know he was home. The last time he texted me was this morning when he sent pictures from the award show after-party. He hadn't mentioned taking an earlier flight or stopping by my uncle's house.

I pushed out a breath while tossing my phone onto the bed. This wouldn't have been such a big deal if I hadn't already made plans for us. I knew things wouldn't change overnight. That was an absurd wish. But, I expected a genuine effort from both sides. Sergio wasn't making this easy for me.

Before taking off my dress, I snapped a picture for Sergio. He needed to see what he missed out on tonight. Maybe next time he'd check in before making plans. I sent the pictures, then did a second pass in my closet. After settling on a casual dress and heels, I touched up my makeup. I was tempted to wash it all off as it was too much for dinner, but I liked the smokey eye and red lipstick pairing.

While waiting for the driver to arrive, I carefully placed Sergio's gift on his nightstand. Sergio had wanted a Piaget Polo watch for a while now. I had my personal shopper searching all over for the one with the sapphire crystal face. This was supposed to be his anniversary gift, but it was on backorder. When she called me yesterday, saying she found one, I wasted no time approving the purchase.

I hoped to give it to him tonight at dinner. Just before our dessert arrived, I planned to place the black leather box on the table. I shook my head while adjusting the cobalt blue bow that was affixed to the box. The sound of my phone ringing prompted me to grab my purse and keys. Minutes later, I was hopping into an all-black truck. I hadn't even settled in my seat before my phone chimed. I smirked when I saw Sergio's contact picture. After declining the call, I sat back in my seat, satisfied.

It's too late to call now.

"DON'T YOU LOOK BEAUTIFUL," Denice said after opening the door. She stepped back to fully take in my appearance. I bit my bottom lip to fight back my smile.

"Thank you," I replied while hugging her. "Where are the guys?"

"They're in Mike's office."

We walked to the kitchen. I scanned the island, quickly concluding what was for dinner, lasagna. The smell of Denice's spice blend filled the air, making my stomach growl. She checked the food through the oven window before washing lettuce from her garden..

"I'll let your uncle tell you all the details, but the guys will be pretty busy over the next five years."

My eyes widened. "What do you mean?"

"I don't want to spoil the surprise." She grabbed a wineglass from the cabinet. "Want some?" Her gaze fell on the opened bottle of cabernet on the counter. I nodded.

"You can't leave me hanging like that, Niecy."

She laughed. "So, Mike signed a five-year deal with Warner Media. Part of that deal includes Sergio producing and directing projects. Again, I'll let him tell you all the details, but yeah. I think they're having a celebratory cigar as we speak."

"Good for them," I mused, then sipped my wine.

"You okay, Mick? Your energy seems a little off." Denice's eyes narrowed, daring me to say otherwise. With her hands on her hips, she asked, "What's going on with you?"

She moved to the opposite counter to cut vegetables for a garden salad. I made myself comfortable, taking a seat at the kitchen island and watched her work. After another swig of wine, I placed the glass down on the marble countertops.

Moments like this made me miss my parents even more. How did they overcome issues in their marriage? I always wondered if my mom's straightforwardness was too much for my dad. Did they always confront their issues head on? This was advice I could've used from my mom.

Denice was the next best thing, and I knew she would keep this conversation between us. I appreciated Kamryn's advice, but her husband wasn't in the industry. There were nuances she'd never understand; like the reasons Sergio and I wedded in the first place.

"How do you deal with my uncle's busy schedule? I

mean, he takes breaks, but when he's in grind mode, nothing else matters. Does that not bother you?"

Denice wiped her hands on her apron while walking over to me. "It bothered me in the beginning, but I think he's figured out a good work-life balance. Are things okay with you and Sergio? I know he has a lot going on. Just remember, every decision he makes has you in mind."

I chuckled mirthlessly. "I don't know about that."

The concern in her brown eyes had me breaking eye contact to look off into the distance.

"Oh, baby." She cupped my cheek, bringing my gaze back to hers. "Have you talked about it?"

"Yes, recently."

"And no change?"

"We're figuring it out," I replied with a shrug. "This year has been one project after the next. With this deal, it'll only get busier."

Denice met my gaze and flashed me a sympathetic smile. "Yes, it is. Sergio loves his work, but he loves you more. Like life, relationships have their ebbs and flows. But you guys will be fine. Trust me."

I wanted to believe her, but he couldn't do something as simple as calling when he landed. The deal my uncle signed was major, but still, he should've let me know he made it safe and sound.

"Trust what?" The sound of Uncle Mike's baritone made me jump in my seat. He walked over to me and planted a kiss on my forehead. "My Mickey. How are you, baby?"

I smiled, feeling like a kid again. "I'm good. How about you?"

"I'm great. I have news to share at dinner. Baby, where's that bottle of vintage Moët?"

Denice smiled. "In the cellar."

"Hey, Mick," came from the doorway. Butterflies flooded my belly at the sight of Sergio. He leaned against the doorframe with a grin. His hands were in the pockets of his joggers, and his baseball cap was backwards.

"Hey," I said to him, trying my hardest to seem unmoved by his presence. When all I wanted to do was run over to him and cover his face with a million kisses.

"Can I talk to you for a sec?"

I turned to Denice, who motioned for me to go. When I was within his reach, Sergio hooked his arm around my waist, pulling me flush with his body. I drew in a sharp breath before looking into his eyes. His smirk was boyish. I hated the way my insides danced when he looked at me this way. He missed me just as much as I missed him. I melted in his arm.

"Okay, lovebirds," my uncle groused from behind. I glanced over my shoulder in time to catch him kissing Denice on the neck.

"You're one to talk," I replied, then turned my attention back to Sergio. He released my waist to take me by the hand.

"What happened to the red dress?" He peered down at me, amusement danced in his eyes.

I bit my lip and looked away. "Changed my mind."

Sergio pulled me into the formal living and closed the door behind him. "I should've called sooner."

"Correct." I crossed my arms.

Sergio ran his hand over his face. "I caught an earlier

flight to surprise you but when I landed I saw Mike had been blowing me up about the deal. I expected to be here for an hour, tops."

My heart softened after hearing he changed his flight for me. However, I couldn't let him off too easily.

"A text would've sufficed."

He nodded. "You're right. There's no excuse, really."

A smile covered my face before I could help it. Sergio was so cute in his joggers, hoodie, and baseball cap. It was nothing special, just his typical travel attire.

"I made reservations at our favorite restaurant," I told him while walking over to him.

Sergio's gaze skirted over me, and he licked his lips. "I guess I'll need to make it up to you, huh? I made us miss our reservations, and I missed the chance to see you in that red dress."

"Yup," I said while wrapping my arms around his neck. "But tell me more about you leaving Dallas early."

"After the show, I went out with some colleagues. Seeing everyone with their spouses made me wonder why you weren't there with me. Francis, Joey, and Preston all asked about you, by the way."

I licked my lips. "I have a job now, so I can't travel everywhere with you."

Last year, I quit my job after realizing how unhappy I was working solely in a lab. For six months, I traveled almost everywhere with Sergio. I enjoyed our time together, and it gave me a better understanding of his role in the industry. He was more than a child-star turned director. His colleagues and friends revered him.

Bringing me along also gave our marriage more

authenticity. We weren't dumb. We knew people questioned our union. Even though we had fallen in love by then, there were people who weren't convinced. I went through the usual tabloid hazing. I was called a gold digger. They brought up my past relationships to the light, and people searched for a reason to make me the villain in Sergio's life.

Most of the information came from obsessed fans. Other sources came from his "friends" who'd "known" him for most of his life. I took all the backlash to the chin because I expected pushback. It was the norm in this industry. Building relationships with his circle was important to him and our marriage, therefore it was important to me. I enjoyed every minute of that time, but my ambition wouldn't allow me to settle for being a trophy wife.

During my break from work, I was still actively creating content and posting regularly on social media. My expertise led to Kamryn bringing me on as a brand ambassador. When Kamryn and her former business partner parted ways because of creative differences, I stepped up as the assistant manager temporarily.

"Yeah, but your hours are flexible, right? And your meetings are mostly virtual. We can work it out where you *can* travel with me."

I removed my arms from around his neck. My stomach churned as I realized what was happening.

"I don't know, Serg."

His eyebrows furrowed. "Why not? We want to spend more time together. That's an obvious solution, I think."

My lips parted, but nothing came out. How was I going

to tell him I didn't like constantly traveling and adjusting to time differences? Jet Setting was fun in the beginning because it was new, but I didn't want that to become my norm.

There was a knock at the door, saving me from this topic. "Dinner is ready. I'm moving everything to the dining room," Denice said from the hallway.

The door opened, and my uncle eyed us. "What y'all doing in here?"

I grabbed Sergio's hand and pulled him into the hallway. "Talking."

"Did you spoil the surprise?" Uncle Mike looked at Sergio with wide eyes.

"No, he didn't," I replied with a smile.

"Good. Let's go eat."

We hung back while my uncle walked toward the dining room. I interlocked my fingers with Sergio, sensing a change in his mood.

"We can finish this later," I told him.

Sergio nodded. "Okay."

He released my hand and walked toward the dining room. I stood in the hallway, confused by the sudden change of events. Before I could think too deeply into it, I joined everyone at the dinner table. Sergio sat across from me and avoided eye contact as my uncle tore the foil covering from his bottle of champagne. Denice's eyes bounced from me to Sergio. I looked down at the ivory and gold plating Denice used to set the table.

"Mickey, today I signed a five-year, seven-figure deal with Warner Media." My Uncle's smile warmed my heart. "There's no group of people that I'd rather celebrate with more than the three of you." He looked at me, Sergio, and then Denice. "This deal will secure our future, and y'all's children's futures."

My stomach twisted at the mention of children. I looked at Sergio, who was nodding his head. We talked about expanding our family earlier this year. So much had happened since our last conversation. I wasn't sure where he stood on the matter anymore. The sharp sound of the cork popping snapped me from my thoughts.

"To building a legacy," my uncle said after filling everyone's glasses.

I lifted my glass toward him. "Cheers."

Sergio and I locked gazes. There was a smile on his face, but the happiness didn't meet his eyes. My eyebrows met as I tried to communicate with him from across the table. He gave me nothing. I brought my champagne glass to my lips and took a long sip.

Ebb and flow

CHAPTER FIVE

Sergio

I CHECKED the time on my watch. The sapphire blue crystal face gleamed under the lighting in the kitchen. I smiled, feeling grateful for receiving such a thoughtful gift from Michaela. When we returned from her uncle's, it was waiting on my nightstand. She stood in the doorway of her closet as I opened the small box. My eyebrows rose and mouth slacked when I saw what was inside.

"Welcome home," she said with a smirk.

I removed the watch from the box and slid it onto my wrist. After securing the clasp, I walked over to her and kissed her. I cupped her cheeks, tilting her head back to meet my gaze. She grabbed my hands, turning to kiss my palm.

I hadn't forgotten about the conversation at her uncle's place. It bothered me how easily she shot down the idea of traveling with me. Having her by my side at work events and business dinners was an indescribable feeling. Doing it alone was lonely, especially when everyone else had their partners and spouses with them. Now wasn't the time to address it, though. I wanted to enjoy this moment with her.

"Thank you, baby."

I trailed kisses down her neck while raising her dress over her hips. Dropping to my knees, I met her center. She held my shoulder for support while I removed her panties. She smiled down at me as I kissed her inner thigh and the moist folds of her pussy.

The first swipe of my tongue made her moan. The second and third had her eyes closing and head falling back. I sucked slowly, pulling a husky groan from her. She raked her hands through my fade, uttering incoherent praises. I smirked, pleased with the wetness spilling from between her thighs. I pressed my face deeper into her pussy, savoring in the sweetness of her juices. I didn't let up until she had her fill. Afterward, we moved to the bed where I expressed to her my undying gratitude until we were too spent to move.

For the past week, I'd been thinking of gifts that could top this watch. In the meantime, I made reservations at a new restaurant for Thanksgiving. Neither of us wanted to hire a chef, and nor did we want the traditional holiday meal. I walked to the staircase and listened for Michaela's footsteps.

"Mick," I yelled. "We need to leave, baby."

"I'm coming," she said back.

I chuckled at the quickness of her cadence as she stalked the hallway. Licking my lips, I watched as Michaela sauntered down the steps. Her eyes locked with mine; fire danced in her coffee orbs. I held back a chuckle, wondering if we'd even make it to dinner. My eyes fell on the diamond necklace adorning her chest. The stones looked magnificent against her mocha brown skin. Michaela was a sight, and it didn't matter how many times I watched her make an entrance; I was blown away every time. The red, off-the-shoulder dress complemented Michaela's slender frame and stressed her curves. A smile tugged at the corners of her mouth once she reached the bottom step.

"Hey, beautiful."

I dropped a kiss on her lips, careful not to smudge her lipstick. She swiped my bottom lip with her thumb while giggling.

"You still haven't told me where we're going."

"It's somewhere new." Michaela smiled, revealing those dimples I loved. My groin tightened.

"Yeah, that really narrows it down," she said.

I kissed her on the forehead. "You'll know soon enough."

Thirty minutes later, we arrived at the restaurant to a few paparazzi on the sidewalk. Since I was a teen, the paparazzi had been capturing my every move. I used to do crude shit like flash them the finger. Those pictures always earned one of Big Mama's fussing. The more I matured, the more I realized, if I left them alone, they'd do the same for me. Now, I breezed past them without acknowledgement. Paparazzi didn't even bother talking to me.

Michaela hadn't gotten used to having her pictures taken and questions being yelled her way. I hurried to open the car door for Michaela and pulled her close to my side. She gripped my shirt as we walked into the lavish restaurant. Ambient music replaced the sounds of shutter clicks and camera flashes.

"You okay?" I asked, before kissing her temple.

She nodded. "I'm fine."

A host greeted us and then escorted us to our booth. Soft yellow lights illuminated the room as we weaved through tables. Couples spoke in hushed tones over a candle lit dinners. Once we reached our U-shaped booth, Michaela slid in first. I followed and then retrieved the menu from the host.

"Tia was just telling me about this place," Michaela said while skimming the menu.

I smirked. "Yeah. Me too."

Our eyes met, and the corners of her mouth lifted.

"Complimentary champagne?" The server placed two flutes onto the cloth-covered table. I nodded my thanks before he moved to the next table.

I handed Michaela the first flute, then picked up the other one.

"Happy Thanksgiving, baby."

Michaela grinned. "Happy Thanksgiving."

An hour later, we shared a slice of cake and ice cream

while Michaela recapped her latest video shoot. This week we worked from home, and Michaela recorded a month's worth of content in her greenhouse. She contracted The Jones Collective, my creative agency, to record and edit videos for social media. I stopped by briefly to make sure everything was going according to plan. Watching Michaela care for her plants pulled at my heartstrings. There was a warmth in her eyes and passion behind her words whenever she spoke about the greenhouse. I was happy she'd found her calling.

"Enough about work," Michaela said after a moment. "What are we going to do in Beaver Creek for ten days? Should I bring all of your gifts, or just a few?" She tilted her head to the side and grinned.

I sat back in my seat while wiping the corners of my mouth. "Go skiing, shop, eat, sleep, and whatever else you want to do. I'm looking forward to having you to myself."

Placing my hand on her thigh, I gave it a gentle squeeze.

"Are you sure you want to go skiing?" Michaela asked between giggles. "Remember what happened the last time?"

"Okay. We'll go snow tubing then."

"Yeah, you're less likely to sprain an ankle that way."

I leaned in, brushing my nose along her neck. "You got jokes tonight; I see."

Michaela angled her head, aligning her lips with mine. She pressed her mouth against mine before pulling back.

"Thank you for tonight," she said, meeting my gaze. I inhaled a deep breath as heat shot through me. Her smile was addicting. I was willing to do whatever to keep one on her face.

"You're welcome, baby."

Her lips found mine for an endearing kiss. I cupped her cheek, holding her in place as I pecked and sucked her lips. Her tongue met mine and gave it a teasing lap. I groaned, wanting more of her heady kisses. The warmth of her lips and the sweetness of vanilla ice cream that lingered on them had me kissing her harder. My pulse quickened when she moaned into my mouth. She pulled away; her stare was as hot as molten lava.

"Should I get the check?"

Michaela smirked. "Yeah, you should."

I STARED out the window at the blanket of snow covering the mountains in the distance. People were already on the slopes, skiing and snowboarding in the powdery snow. Another wave of flakes started about an hour ago. I noticed after taking a break from reading Mecca's script. After talking to Michael about the Warner Media deal, I was considering pitching Mecca's movie to them.

We had a long way to go before that point, but I could see the potential. I hadn't been this excited about a project that wasn't mine since reading Tia's script. I wished her debut would've received more support from the studio. When I brought them the idea, I knew they only moved forward because of me. Their financial support was minimal, leaving me and Michael to make up the difference. *Out of Luck* had limited viewings in theater.

There were a lot of factors that were out of our control. I'd never let that happen again. Tia deserved more, and I was determined to make it happen.

The sound of Michaela's footsteps padding across the room snapped me from my trance. I sipped my lukewarm coffee while watching her make the bed.

"Good morning, sleepyhead."

She rolled her eyes at me. "We got here super late last night, Serg."

"Hey, it wasn't my fault," I noted.

Michaela had a last-minute meeting that went over, forcing us to catch a later flight. Unfortunately, the only first-class seats available were on the last flight. By the time we checked in at the resort, it was after midnight. We ordered food from a nearby restaurant for dinner. An hour later, Michaela was asleep. I expected her to wake up at sunrise, ready to start the day. It was a quarter to eleven when she finally stirred.

"Wanna grab something from the café?" I asked as she disappeared into the bathroom.

"Sounds good," she replied as the door closed. Minutes later, she emerged from the bathroom while drying her face with a towel. After discarding it in the hamper outside of the closet, she removed her scarf to comb her hair. I watched Michaela as she styled her hair in the standing mirror outside of the bathroom door. Dressed in a navy pajama set that matched mine, she was a beauty.

"Today is the perfect day for snow tubing," she mused. She met me near the window and sat on the arm of my chair. I draped my arm around her waist and pulled her onto my lap.

"We can do whatever you want. But we have to be back by four o'clock," I said after a moment.

"Why?" she asked while squirming my arms. I peppered kisses along her cheek until I met her lips. "I was thinking we could go to the lodge for cookies and hot cocoa afterward."

"We can have cookies and hot cocoa here while we decorate the Christmas tree."

Michaela's eyes lit up, and the sweetest grin covered her face. "You got us a tree?"

"Yup. Ornaments, lights, ribbons; the whole nine."

She wrapped her arms around my neck. The warmth from her body sent a shiver through me. I tightened my hold on her waist, drawing her body closer to mine. I inhaled a deep breath. We remained in this position for a few seconds. The sound of Michaela's stomach growling made me chuckle.

"Let's get dressed," I said with a chuckle.

After eating at the cafe, we rode the ski lift up the mountain. The views were spectacular. The snow was so white; it was damn near blinding. Michaela was on the edge of her seat, snapping pictures with a grin. We wore matching all black ski suits and boots, compliments of my wife. She'd bought them a few days before the trip, along with a few sets of matching pajamas. I was certain the pajamas were for Christmas.

"OMG!" Michaela squealed. "Look what Reyla just sent me."

My eyebrows shot up when she handed me her phone. A fashion blog wrote a piece on Michaela and her best outfits of the year. The infamous red dress made the list.

Pictures of us entering Catch LA on Thanksgiving were posted on their social media and website. They also included pictures of her walking with Kamryn into The Plant Shop, and snapshots from her YouTube videos. Overall, it was a great piece that showcased her style.

"This is good, baby. Why the frown?"

She blew out a breath before biting her bottom lip. "I don't like things like this. You're the star. The spotlight doesn't need to be on me."

"Unfortunately, it doesn't work like that."

"I stay in my lane and out of the way. I don't need another incident like before."

"That won't happen again."

"How do you know?"

I sighed. "Because I made sure it wouldn't."

A group of my former friends, including the star of my debut movie, Azra Livingston, sent fake stories to gossip blogs to tarnish my wife's reputation. My PR team didn't have to do much to get the stories taken down, but the damage had been done. Michaela had internalized the lies. The whole ordeal left a sour taste in her mouth. She hated the paparazzi and hated being in the blogs, even if it showed her in a positive light.

"We'll see, I guess." Michaela put her phone away and stared out the window. I grabbed her by the hand, forcing her to meet my gaze.

"I know it's a lot sometimes, but it's what comes with the territory. You have over one-hundred and fifty thousand followers and are married to someone who's been in the spotlight for most of their life; you're going to have eyes on you. It's overwhelming, I know. But you can control how people view you."

"No, I can't. You saw what happened last time."

"The content you create and partnerships you've established are two examples. You can become a style influencer too, if you want. It seems people like your sense of fashion," I told her with a wink.

"Whatever, Serg." A smile broke on her pretty face, making warmth spread in my chest. "We're almost at the top. Want to make a friendly bet before we get out?"

"What were you thinking?"

An impish smirk covered her lips. *This was going to be good.*

"The loser has to cook Christmas dinner."

"Or make dinner reservations. Mick, you know I can't cook."

"Are you claiming defeat already?"

I chuckled. "Not at all. Just trying to make sure we have a good holiday; in the rare case I lose."

She held out her hand. "Fine. Let's shake on it."

"YOU CHEATED, but It's cool. I'll make reservations somewhere nice."

Michaela glanced over her shoulder and laughed. "Don't be a sore loser."

I couldn't prove it, but Michaela's "snow tube expert" used extra force when pushing her over the ledge. The first race, she was down the hill by the time I was even pushed. I won the second time, making the third race an intense one. Michaela gripped the handles on her tube tightly and straightened her posture. She eyed me with a smirk, mouthing the word, "loser," before zipping down the hill. I was too busy laughing at her to brace myself before being thrust down the hill.

To make matters worse, my tube spun around. I had to finish the race backwards. Once I reached the bottom, I ran over to Michaela and tackled her into a mound of snow. She laughed hysterically. Seeing her so happy was infectious and soon I joined in on the laughter.

I missed this side of us. The happy, carefree couple we were in the beginning. Everything was so new, so eye-opening, that I dared not miss a moment. We made time for each other, talked about everything, and had the entire world before us. It hadn't been a full-day, and I was already feeling closer to Michaela.

After our race, we watched other couples race before returning to our cabin. Our concierge facilitated the tree and ornament delivery while we were away. All that was left to do was decorate it.

"Want to order a dozen cookies from the café? They have a lot of options." Michaela waved the menu at me. "What's on your mind?"

Walking over to her, I wrapped my arms around her waist.

"Nothing. Just how much I love you."

She smiled. "I love you too."

An hour later, I was on the couch near the fireplace drinking sugary sweet cocoa. Michaela held up a sparkly gold ornament and a shiny navy ornament. Her eyes glistened, and a small smile formed on her lips. Mariah

Carey's Christmas album played in the background, and another wave of snowfall had just begun. The seven-foot artificial Noble Fir tree was placed in front of our living room window overlooking the courtyard. Once decorated, I knew it would be a sight with the snowy mountains in the background. It was the perfect holiday scene.

"How does navy and gold sound?" My gaze fell on Michaela in her black and red plaid pajamas. She stared at me wistfully, then said, "The last Christmas I spent with my parents we decorated the tree with those colors. My mom had this beautiful satin ribbon she wrapped around the tree with the lights. It was really pretty."

"I like navy and gold."

After separating the ornaments she wanted from the bins, we began decorating. We'd stop occasionally to view the tree, dance, or eat a cookie or two. By the time we finished, it was dark enough to light the tree. I plugged in the soft white lights and adjusted the twinkle setting. We decided on the slowest pattern; the lights alternated by rows, flowing like the snowflakes outside.

"It's beautiful," Michaela marveled with glimmering eyes. I walked over to Michaela and stood behind her. She angled her head to meet my gaze.

"Yeah, it is," I said, then kissed her on the cheek.

CHAPTER SIX

Michaela

OUR CABIN WAS EERILY QUIET. I unzipped my coat and slipped off my boots before venturing to the living room. It was empty, showing no signs of my husband anywhere.

I noticed more boxes under the tree and made a mental note to call the wrapping station after I showered. Before my workout, I dropped off Sergio's gifts. We planned to open everything tonight. Tomorrow we would go see the Christmas lights after dinner.

I gripped the banister as I climbed the stairs leading to our bedroom. My legs were sore and core ached from an intense pilates class. I received a flyer for the class yesterday while leaving the spa and decided to attend.

As intense as the class was, it also gave me a chance to think. The past three days with Sergio had been perfect. From snow tubing to decorating the three, it felt like the spark was back. We spent the past two days in our cabin watching movies, trying recipes from TikTok, and just enjoying each other's company. I missed talking to Sergio. The quick "how's work" check ins had become so mundane and expected that I dreaded the topic. I had become so detached from his work.

During my workout, I realized I contributed to the disconnect between us. I stopped visiting him at his office and tagging along for work trips. Tia used to block off lunch dates for us, some Sergio knew about ahead of time; others were spontaneous. Before he left for Italy, his workload forced him to work through lunch and sometimes dinner, too. One canceled lunch date turned into four canceled dates. If I had been more communicative about why I visited less, maybe we could've found solutions sooner. Him being in Italy for two and a half months only made the distance worse.

I concluded that he needed reassurance just as much as I did. Our marriage wasn't a simple agreement anymore. I cherished what we had. He needed to know how committed I was to us.

When I reached the top of the stairs, I noticed the door to our insulated balcony was cracked. I smiled after finding Sergio in the lounge chair, wholly engrossed in his tablet. His long, slim frame took over the cream-colored chair. He'd tossed the decorative pillows onto the floor to make more room. Dressed in an all gray sweatsuit, he looked so at peace, so cozy. I, on the other hand, felt like I'd run a 5K race.

"I thought we said no work during this trip."

He looked up from his tablet and smirked. "I was waiting for you to return. Come here."

After placing the tablet on the table beside him, he sat upright and reached out for me. I walked over to him without hesitation. The warmth in his eyes had me quickening my strides.

"I'm sweaty," I whined when he pulled me onto him.

"So," he crooned in my ear.

"What are you reading?"

He picked up his tablet and showed me the first page of the script.

"The Come Up. Hmm," I hummed. "What's it about?"

Sergio gave me a short spiel of the movie before saying, "When we get home, I'm going to set up a meeting with Mecca. I'm thinking about funding it myself and asking Tia if she wants to direct."

"Tia?"

Sergio's eyebrows met. "Yeah. She loves the story, and she deserves it after what happened with the first movie."

I caressed the top of his head. "Are you sure Tia's ready for another movie? She was pretty down after *Out of Luck*'s reviews came out."

"Did she say something to you?"

Biting my lip, I looked away. "Not exactly. She wants more time to hone her craft. Maybe shadow you and other directors for a bit."

"She hasn't said anything to me about it."

"Give her the chance to."

He shook his head. "I don't know, Mick. I've been waiting for a year for her to say something. She jumped back into being an assistant, and while I appreciate having her, she's destined for greatness."

"I agree, but you can't rush her."

Sergio looked at me; those sienna orbs made me weak in the knees, still. "It's Christmas Eve and I've somehow found a way to talk about work." He chuckled. "How was Pilates?"

"It was really good. I can't wait to get back in the studio at home."

"Why'd you stop?"

"Kamryn was my Pilates partner and since she's pregnant," I trailed off.

He laughed while shaking his head. "I'm sure you're pretty sore, huh?"

I squirmed in his lap when he squeezed my thigh. "Very."

"I got something for the soreness." He nodded toward the door leading to our bathroom.

I stood from his lap to go see what he'd done. My hand flew to my mouth when I walked into the bathroom. The shades were halfway down, and the lights were on the lowest setting. In the center of the bathroom was a double slipper tub. Surrounding the tub were candles, roses, and a bottle of champagne on ice. The rose petals formed a path from the door to the bathtub. I leaned over, noting the petals at the bottom.

"You like it?" Sergio was on my heels, waiting for my reaction.

"I love it."

He reached around me to turn on the water. I shuddered a sigh when he dropped a quick peck on the curve of my neck. Goosebumps covered my skin from the tender kiss. He sat along the side of the tub to adjust the water's temperature before filling it. Once the tub was halfway, he added bath salts and bubble bath to the water. The smell of lavender wafted from the tub as a mass of foam formed.

While the water ran, I peeled off my leggings, followed by my sports bra and tank top. I pulled my hair into a high bun before sitting on the edge across from Sergio. He eyed me hungrily from head to toe. The look in his eyes hit me right in-between the legs. I reached for the hem of his sweatshirt and pulled it over his head.

"Join me," I purred in his ear, earning a throaty chuckle from him. He held my hand, assisting me as I got into the tub. Once I was settled, I nodded toward the opposite side of the tub. "There's more than enough room for you."

"This is supposed to be for you."

"But I want you in here with me." I fluttered my lashes and tilted my head to the side. "We've been here for three days and haven't used the tub yet."

Sergio stared at me with furrowed eyebrows. He was trying to convince himself not to go in the tub. A smirk covered my lips as I sunk into the water and kicked water his way.

"Are you really going to deny me?"

"You know I'd never do that."

"So, why are you still standing there?"

With a smirk, Sergio removed his sweatpants then

joined me in the tub. There was just enough space for him to stretch his legs on either side of me. I rested my legs over his and leaned against the back of the tub. Our gazes locked. Heat rushed my body, forcing me to look away. I had to tell him what I was thinking, but I didn't want to kill the vibe.

"What's going on, Mick?" he asked with pensive eyes. I looked away while treading my hands through the bubbly water. "I know when there's a million thoughts racing through your mind," he added.

A cheek lifted as I fought back a grin. "I want to talk to you about something, but I don't want to ruin this moment."

"You won't," he assured me.

"I'll start by saying how much I'm enjoying this time with you, and I don't want it to end."

"But?"

I licked my lips. "But I'm wondering how we can keep this energy. I know how much your career means to you, and I never want you to feel guilty about working. However, I need to feel like a priority too. We used to have lunch dates at the office, and somehow, meetings stole my afternoon slots."

Sergio's eyebrows furrowed as he recollected the instances where he had canceled at the last minute.

"I never addressed it because I thought it would be temporary. It's been eight months since I last visited you at the office. Me not speaking up caused this rift between us. I don't want us to grow to resent each other."

Sergio looked away, and I could tell his mind was racing. He lifted his arms from the water and placed them on either side of the tub. I drew in a sharp breath when he looked at me. His eyes narrowed like he was trying to figure out a puzzle or something. When his pensive gaze became too much to bear, my gaze lowered to his chest. I stared at the tattoo on his left pectoral.

My initials were inscribed in courier font, the font used when screenwriting, near his heart. He said it was an ode to his two loves: me and film. I got our anniversary tattooed on my right ankle with ivy vines underneath. We'd gotten them randomly last summer after returning home from Las Vegas. There was something thrilling about getting matching tattoos on impulse. The moment was also sentimental since they were our first and only tattoos.

Things like that reminded me how deeply connected Sergio and I were. Our love story wasn't ideal, but the bond we'd built was impenetrable. The mere thought of Sergio and not working out triggered knots in my stomach.

"I've been thinking about that a lot too," he confessed moments later. "When we talked about getting married, I did not know my life would become all this. My number one goal was to get out of that situation to save my career. I knew I could trust you. More than anything, I expected for us to become great friends. I got that and more. Mick, I want this to work." There was a pang in my chest from the longing in his tone. "I need this to work because you're the best thing that has ever happened to me. I wouldn't have any of this without you. Whatever I need to do, I'll do."

My eyes stung with tears.

"When we get back home, I talk to Tia about blocking off lunch times for us. I'll try not to schedule meetings too late in the evening. As far as workload, I can make adjustments there too. There will be opportunities that will require me to be away for months at a time. I need to know that you'll be flexible with your schedule."

"I will, but it's a lot, Serg."

He rubbed my thighs. "I know, baby. It's my fault for not easing you into this lifestyle. We came into this shit so blindly." Sergio shook his head while chuckling. "We talked about the future, but we didn't really plan for it, huh?"

I shook my head. "Not at all.

"They always said marriage required sacrifice and compromise."

"Yup, and communication."

Sergio's mouth curved into a half smile. His gaze fell on my left knee, where he traced small circles with his index finger. I inched my foot up his thigh, pulling a deep sigh from him. Just when I reached his crotch, he pulled my foot. Our bodies met in the middle of the tub. Water and bubbles sloshed, hitting the floor on all sides. I belted a laugh while throwing my arms around his neck. My insides warmed from his possessive hold on my butt.

He ravished my lips, leaving me breathless. Our tongues danced slowly as we savored each other. He pulled away to look at me. My stomach fluttered at the love in his eyes. His hand moved from my ass to my breast. Taking my nipple between his index and thumb, twisted it sending waves of pleasure through me.

"I love you, Michaela," he rasped.

I brushed my lips against his before taking his bottom lip into my mouth. His groan sent a chill down my spine.

"I love you too, baby," I replied.

Sergio smiled against my lips while lifting me onto his erection. He captured my lip between his, giving it a gentle suck. Slowly, he lowered me onto him. I sighed while wrapping my legs around him. More water spilled from the tub as I rolled my hips over him. Sergio held me close, my chest pressed against his as our bodies moved as one. His groans were so intoxicating and sexy. I rocked faster, not caring about the water we'd have to clean up afterward.

My lips parted, and a whimper spilled from my lips. Sergio's eyebrows furrowed and his sienna orbs darkened. The intensity in his eyes was arresting. I loved when he looked at me this way. I could see the deep love he had for me in them. With his lip tucked between his teeth, he thrusted upward. I grabbed the sides of the tub while winding my waist over him. My stomach tightened when he pecked my neck. His hot, hungry kisses sent me over the edge.

"Ahh," I cried out. He thrusted faster and harder, our bodies moved against the waves of the water. Sergio chuckled throatily and held me tighter. Waves of ecstasy ripped through me from his touch.

"There you go, baby," he praised. "Just like that." I rocked my hips until a downpour of fiery sensations coursed through me. Sergio's eyes remained on me as I unraveled in his arms. The smallest, sexiest smirk curved his mouth. I closed my eyes and threw back my head, fully submitting to another orgasm.

"Look at me, Mick," Sergio rasped. My eyes sprung open in time to see his undoing. "It's you and me, baby."

I nodded; a bevy of emotions boiled in my belly. With furrowed eyebrows and flared nostrils, he released a satisfying grunt. I loved this man with everything in me. I crashed my mouth into his for one last kiss.

The kiss was slow, intimate, and hot enough to start *another* round.

"IT'S ALMOST MIDNIGHT," Sergio crooned in my ear. We'd just finished watching *Home Alone 2: Lost in New York*. The lights of the Christmas tree illuminated Sergio's caramel colored skin, making my heart flutter. He looked so fine in his black silk pajamas and Santa hat.

After our bath, we showered, then ordered food. We took an unexpected nap once we finished eating. I woke up first and was able to sneak away to get Sergio's gifts from the wrapping station. While at the main lodge, I grabbed a bottle of champagne and a charcuterie board. By the time I returned, Sergio was awake and ready to start our Christmas movie binge. We watched *The Preacher's Wife*, *This Christmas*, and ended with my childhood favorite, *Home Alone 2*.

"Want to open your first present?" he asked with a raised eyebrow.

"Yes!" I jumped from our spread on the floor and ran to the tree. "Which one should I open first?"

Sergio joined me by the tree. "The one with the green bow."

I looked at all the gifts, noting the one rectangular box that had a green bow. All the other gifts had red and gold bows. I untied the pretty emerald colored bow and tore the black metallic wrapping paper.

I opened the box to a gold envelope. Meeting Sergio's gaze, I smirked before breaking the seal. I pulled out a card with the words "Happy Anniversary" on the front.

"What is this?" I mused while opening the card. On the inside was a leather map of an island. "Year three will be spent at Happy Island." My eyes widened when I realized what it was. "Rab Island!" I shrieked. Sergio nodded and a wide smile stretched across his face.

Located off the coast of Croatia, Rab Island, also known as 'heaven on earth' was where we wanted to spend our two-year anniversary. We had to postpone the trip after Sergio's film went into production. I had just signed my deal with Green's Love and had meetings to no end. Neither of our schedules allowed for traveling.

A few weeks before our anniversary, we made plans to meet at a central location. We settled on a staycation in Manhattan during his three-day visit to the states. Sergio was exhausted, but he pushed through for our special day.

"Since we couldn't go last year," he told me.

"Thanks, baby. I can't wait," I said while wrapping my arms around his neck.

"Neither can I. Merry Christmas, my love." He kissed my forehead tenderly, causing warmth to fill my cheeks.

"Merry Christmas."

THE SOUND of unfamiliar voices stirred me from my slumber. I turned over to find Sergio's side of the bed empty. I figured he was downstairs with our concierge. She visited twice a day to give us the resort's daily spiel and to ensure everything was to our standards. I still wasn't used to living so luxuriously. Some days, I woke up in awe of the life I lived. So much had transpired, but it wasn't that long ago I was stressed, working several jobs to make ends meet.

I inhaled a deep breath while tossing back the covers. I dreaded this day the most; my parents' death anniversary. My heart ached for my younger self. Losing both parents during my senior year of high school was the worst pain I'd ever felt. For years, I felt lost and alone. I had meaningless relationships and was just merely existing. My college years were a blur. I didn't know if it was repression or if I was that detached from it all. Shaking away those thoughts, I padded to the bathroom.

On my way out of the bathroom, I grabbed my phone off the nightstand. I had several text messages from friends and family members sending me well wishes. I skipped them all to read my uncle's message. He'd visited my parents' gravesites this morning. A picture of a fresh bouquet of white roses on my mother's grave made me teary-eyed. I replied to his message, sending him love, and I promised to call him later. Once I responded to messages from Reyla, Kamryn, and several cousins, I put my phone down.

I descended the stairs to the living room. Sergio was at the coffee table setting up a card and flowers. Another wave of tears pricked my eyes. They were the same roses my uncle had left for my mother. Sergio turned around at the sound of my footsteps. I wiped my cheeks before walking over to him. He said nothing; he just held me tight, providing me the comfort I needed. Nestle in his arms was where I felt at home and safe.

"I miss them," I said after a moment. Sergio kissed the top of my head before cupping my cheek. Angling my head back, I met his worry-filled eyes.

"I know, baby. I wish there was something I could do to take the pain away."

Offering him a wry smirk, I nodded. "Thank you. What's that?"

He stepped aside, giving me a full view of the food he'd ordered for us.

"The flowers are a special delivery from Mike," he said, taking me by the hand. Once we were seated on the couch, Sergio handed me the flowers and the card attached.

I smiled after reading the card from my uncle.

They're smiling down on you, Mickey. Continue to honor them by living out your dreams. Love you.
Uncle Mike.

Pressing the card to my chest, I inhaled a deep breath. When I opened my eyes, Sergio handed me two boxes. I opened the smaller one first. Inside the small velvet box was a gold bracelet with my mother's handwriting engraved on it. My gaze met his as fresh tears fell from my eyes.

In my greenhouse was a framed card my mother gave me during my junior year of high school. I'd always loved her handwriting. Her cursive was precise and extravagant, almost like calligraphy. Whenever she wrote me a note or signed a card, she wrote extensive, heartfelt messages. In This particular, she'd written a paragraph inside, but my favorite part was the last few sentences.

> We're so incredibly proud of you, Mick. Always. You're our greatest joy.
> Soar, baby. Soar.

"Soar, baby. Soar," I read the words that were etched onto my bracelet. Swiping my thumb over the shiny metal, I smirked. "This is perfect." I wondered how he was able to sneak the card without me noticing as I viewed the card almost every day.

Tia.

I shook my head, remembering her stopping by a few days before our trip. She asked me to grab a flower pot from my greenhouse. She must've snapped a picture of the card, too.

Sergio took the bracelet from my hand to put it on my wrist. Once on, I admired it while fighting back tears. This was one of the best gifts he'd given me.

I moved onto the second box, which was larger and heavier too. After tearing through the wrapping paper, I opened the cardboard box. Inside was a snow globe.

"For your collection."

"Couldn't leave without one," I said.

Sergio removed it from the box for me and gave it a

shake. My eyes widened as I watched the snow fall over the small replica of the resort.

"I'll never grow tired of seeing you happy." Sergio squatted in front of me. "I hope our children have the same expression when we show them your collection."

My heart fluttered. "Me too. Remember earlier this year when we said we wanted to try for a baby?"

Sergio nodded. "Yeah, I do. I want it all with you, Michaela. The family, the big house and a thriving career."

"Me too. I have my yearly appointment coming up. I'll talk to my doctor about stopping birth control."

His eyebrows shot up. "I thought you did already?"

"No. Something told me we weren't *really* ready."

The fact that we were talking about it six months later proved we weren't.

He laughed. "Yeah, we needed to work on ourselves first. And we'll continue the work as we start the next journey."

My cheeks hurt from smiling so hard. I couldn't believe we would start our journey to parenthood next year. I didn't always believe I'd find love, but I knew I wanted to be a mother. The idea of loving and nurturing a little being brought me joy. Having Sergio by my side through it all made the dream even sweeter.

Since I moved into his home, he'd gone above and beyond my wildest imagination. Sergio assumed the roles of protector and provider without hesitation. I couldn't wait to see how his loving nature manifests into fatherhood.

After this conversation, I'd somehow fallen in love with him all over again.

CHAPTER SEVEN

Sergio

TIA STRUTTED into my office with coffee in one hand and her tablet in the other. I glanced up from my phone and smiled at her. It was my first day back in the office for the new year. I wanted to complain about the hundreds of emails in my inbox, but I was in too good of a mood to care. Since returning from Beaver Creek, I was still on a high. Michaela did that to me. Ten days with her in the mountains was the reset I needed after a long year.

When we returned home, we kept the romance alive by going on dates every night. I never felt more connected to Michaela. Going away, tuning out all distractions and having tough conversations unlocked a different level of intimacy between us.

"Aw. You're glowing," Tia noted with a smirk. She placed her drink on the corner of my desk before taking a seat.

"Don't start, T. What's on the schedule for the day?" I wiped my hand over my mouth to hide my smile.

Maybe I was "glowing", so what?

She snorted a laugh while looking at her tablet. "Well, you have three meetings before noon. All are phone calls. Oh, Terri called me last night. He wanted me to let you know he's doing okay, and he wants to talk soon. He's in good spirits."

"Cool, cool. I hadn't seen anything in the blogs about him, so that's good. You know where he's been for the last six weeks?"

Tia nodded. "He's checked himself into a rehab facility and started therapy."

Pushing out a breath, I nodded. "I'm glad he got the help he needed."

"Me too. Yema and the other studio heads are also pleased."

I leaned back in my seat while belting out a laugh. "They love talking to you, huh?"

"I'm not sure why," Tia chirped. "Anyway, I'm going to call Mecca and schedule a meeting for next week. I got your notes about his script. I knew you'd love it."

"I did. Speaking of which, how would you feel about giving directing another shot?"

She looked up from her tablet with wide eyes. "I, uh, I thought Mecca wanted *you* to be the director?"

"He does, but I know how much you love this story. I could talk to him about it and see what he thinks. I still plan to rewrite the script and all that. But, T, you've been waiting for your moment, and I believe this is it. "

Tia looked away while chewing her bottom lip. "I don't know, Serg. I'm not sure I'm ready."

"You are."

"*Out of Luck* was a flop. And there were so many reviews noting my inexperience. The studio heads were so hard on me. They set me up for failure. From the production timeline to the rollout, it was all bad. I can't risk messing up Mecca's passion project."

"T, this time will be different. We're not going to a studio for funding. We will make all decisions." I motioned a hand between us. "Mecca just wants the movie made. I can assure him everything will meet his expectations. And that you are the person to do it. I need you to get out of your own way."

"Wow. This was not how I saw the year starting."

"You've been a great assistant to me, but it's time for you to chase your dreams. And I want to do whatever I can to help. This movie is the perfect opportunity for you."

"Why now?"

I shrugged. "You've been holding me down for over a decade. Even when I wasn't working, you showed up everyday for me. I can't continue to hold you back."

Tia deserved to chase her dreams. Being a lowly assistant wasn't the goal when she entered the industry. While I loved having her in my corner, it was time for her to fly. She'd have my full support and *Jones and Watters* would always be her home.

She sniffled, fighting back the tears brimming her hazel eyes. "Sergio, I don't know what to say."

Leaning forward, I drummed my fingers on the desk. "Say you'll do the damn movie."

"Fine. I'll do it." Tia threw up her hands.

"Perfect. Set up the meeting." I moved around my mouse to wake up my computer. "Who am I meeting with first?"

Tia straightened her posture, signaling her switch to professional mode.

"Monroe and Daniel. They want to talk about upcoming projects and budgets."

"Sounds good. Do we have all the documents ready?"

After tapping around on her tablet, she replied, "I just sent them to you. You have twenty minutes to skim over everything."

She stood from her seat. "Thank you for pushing me, Serg. I really appreciate how invested you are in my career."

I waved her off. "Come on, T. We're family. I'll always look out for you."

Tia smiled at me before leaving my office.

RUNNING my hand over my face, I pushed out a breath. I'd just finished my last meeting of the morning and I was exhausted. Standing from my desk, I stretched my limbs before checking my phone. Michaela had texted me pictures of her trying on dresses for the Golden Globe awards next week. I swiped through each picture while smiling. I was glad she didn't ask which I liked because if it were up to me, she'd have them all.

After responding to her text, I checked my calendar to see how long I had to eat lunch. I groaned when I saw Tia had blocked off the next hour-and-a-half for another meeting. Stalking from my desk, I snatched open my door.

"T, what's this on my cal-" I stopped when I saw Michaela and Tia laughing at her desk. They were on Tia's tablet looking at something when I burst out of my office. Tia cleared her throat and put her tablet away.

"Mick asked me to block off lunch for today."

Michaela smirked at me while holding up two bags of food. "Hey."

I couldn't help my smile when I replied, "Hey."

Stepping aside, I nodded for her to enter my office. She sauntered over to me with heated desire in her eyes.

"Thanks, T. I owe you," I told her with a wink.

"Don't you always."

Once inside my office, I locked the door and took Michaela by the waist.

"I'm so happy to see you," I said against her mouth. She kissed me sweetly before taking my bottom lip between her lips.

"I'm even happier to see you." There was a softness in her tone that made my chest tighten. I kissed her again while pulling her body against mine. my stomach growled during our cozy greeting, reminding us why she was here. "Sounds like your stomach is happy I'm here too."

"More like *ecstatic*," I teased. While Michaela made herself comfortable at my desk, I unbagged our food. "You went to my spot." Michaela flashed a beaming smile.

"I did. They've updated the menu since I last visited."

There was a Thai restaurant a few blocks from my office in Hollywood. The staff knew me because I went there for lunch so many times. I put Michaela on a while back and now she was hooked too.

I marveled at the spread of food she'd brought us. Taking a seat next to her, I dug in.

"Which dress did you choose?" I asked between bites.

Michaela finished chewing before answering. "The black chiffon one. The silhouette and side split are my favorites.

"I like it too. I liked them all, actually."

"Me too. I made Rosi choose for me."

"Perks of having a personal shopper, huh?"

She lifted a shoulder, playing coy. "How's your day been so far? Tia said you had meetings all morning."

I blew out a breath. "Back to back to back, Mick. But I won't complain. Monroe and Daniel say we're due for another dinner outing. They'll be in town for the awards show, so we'll plan something then. What about you? What are you and Kamryn up to at The Plant Shop?"

Michaela's eyes widened. "Oh, I have to show you something."

After retrieving her phone from her purse she showed me a picture of a dying plant. The leaves were wilted and some had turned yellow. "What happened to it?"

She giggled. "Kent from Green's Love sent me this in October. This is before they repotted the plant using my soil mix." She swiped to the next picture. "I visited their lab to check on its growth. This is the plant today."

All the leaves were a vibrant green, and the vines had grown tremendously.

"Wow. This doesn't even look like the same plant."

"Right? I can't believe it's thriving like this in just three months. Kamryn says the same happened to a snake plant she has at home."

"So, what's the next phase?"

"They want to run a few more tests, but it's ready for production. My promo shoot is in a few weeks, and the official launch date is June 21st, the Summer Solstice."

"I'll have Tia add it to my calendar."

Michaela smiled. "I'll tell her to add the party too. Did you talk to her about the movie?"

With a nod, I replied, "Yup. It took some convincing, but she'd down to direct. We have a long way to go before we get there, so I'll see if she can shadow a few people before then."

After we finished lunch, I took Michaela to the coffee shop downstairs. I had two more meetings before the end of the day and needed to refuel. She told me about her upcoming doctor's appointment and spa date with Reyla. I was happy to hear their friendship was in a good space. I'd be the first to admit that I was too fond of Reyla before. She came off as selfish, and put Michaela in a dire situation. But if Michaela could forgive her, I could too.

"Well, I have to get to The Plant Shop." Michaela checked the time on her phone. "Amber is stopping by to view the new layout of the store. She and Kamryn decided on having two displays."

"Sounds like they made a great compromise."

She smirked. "Right? Everyone's happy."

We stood from the table to embrace one another.

"I'll see you later, baby."

She kissed my cheek then said, "Later."

THE FLASHING LIGHTS and sounds of cheers were music to my ears. Michaela gripped my hand as we weaved through the bustling red carpet. We were leaving The Golden Globes award for an afterparty in West Hollywood. It was nice to be in the room despite not being nominated. Celebrating the accomplishments of my colleagues never got old.

"Sergio, Sergio! Over here," a camerawoman yelled for my attention. I looked at Michaela whose eyes were wild as she took in the scene. "Just a few more pictures," I said in her ear. Upon our arrival, I had to do a few interviews to promote my upcoming movie, *Burden of Truth*. Michaela stole the show in her gown, garnering a few questions about her career and upcoming projects.

"Besides, everyone deserves to see you in this dress," I added once we stopped.

"Okay, fine," she conceded.

We stopped at the group of photographers and posed. I rested my hand on Michaela's waist. She stepped to the side, exposing the side split of her dress, earning an, "Oooh" from passersby.

"Mrs. Jones, can we get details about the dress?"

Michaela licked her lips before smiling. "It's an Oscar De La Renta."

I stepped back, giving her a moment to show off the

all-black, strapless gown. She wore her hair straight with a middle part, tucked behind her ears. Her make-up was subtle. A little blush on her cheeks with a smokey eye and red lips. She was breathtaking, per usual. After a few more poses, she looked at me for reprieve.

"Thanks everyone. We have to get going," I said, holding Michaela by the small of her back.

They moved on to the next person as we entered our ride for the evening.

"How you feeling?" I asked as we pulled off.

She pushed out a breath. "I'm okay."

My phone had been vibrating nonstop since I took it off silent. While I answered my missed texts and emails, Michaela did the same.

"Would you all like music?" The driver asked.

"No, we're good," I replied, meeting Michaela's eyes. We could use a moment of silence after the award show. I appreciated these moments of stillness now more than ever. In a few minutes, we'd be at a party where I'd have to charm and schmooze my way around the room.

"Oh my God," Michaela shrieked, effectively breaking the silence.

"What's wrong baby?"

"Nothing's wrong. Kamryn decided on her next assistant manager. She's sending the offer letter tomorrow." Her coffee brown eyes gleamed with excitement.

I smiled. "That's great news. What does that mean for you?"

"I'll help with the onboarding and training of the new person. But it means I can focus on the brand and driving sales. No more going to the shop everyday." She sounded a little sad, but quickly recovered with, "More time to travel with you, though."

Her penetrating gaze met mine. Reaching for her hand, I brought it to my lips for a kiss. The bracelet I gifted her dangled from her wrist, catching my attention. She'd worn it every day since receiving it.

Memories of our trip came to mind and I smiled. Two weeks later, I was still riding high from our trip. We weren't in our honeymoon phase any more and we damn sure weren't in the terrible twos. We'd figured out how to balance it all; work, friends, our marriage, and I couldn't be happier. I realized I couldn't rely on the chemistry we had to sustain us. I had to love her with intention, make time for her, and show her how much she meant to me every chance I got. Michaela was a gem. I'd be a fool to lose her.

"I love you, Mrs. Jones" I told her after a moment.

She smiled. "And I love you, Mr. Jones."

CHAPTER EIGHT

Michaela

STANDING NEXT to an all-white G-wagon Mercedes truck, Reyla texted on her phone. She dressed casually for our spa date, wearing a hoodie and jeans. I knew Reyla well enough to know everything was designer. She was in town for the weekend to pick up her wedding dress. Since her wedding was a few weeks away, it was the perfect time for our spa date.

I was excited to see her. It had been months since we had an outing together. Whenever we saw each other, it wasn't long enough. I looked forward to spending time with her in Napa before the ceremony.

"When did you get this?" I asked, getting her attention.

Reyla looked up from her phone and grinned. "An engagement gift from Simon. I couldn't wait to show you."

We shared an earnest embrace before getting in the car. Once inside, Reyla gave me a quick tour of her truck. Simon made sure she had every upgrade possible. The truck came fully equipped with premium leather seats, a panoramic sunroof, and an elaborate LED ambient lighting system. She changed the colors a few times before settling on purple.

"Simon went all out."

She nodded. "He did. I don't know how I can top this gift."

"Yeah. I don't know either," I said, then laughed. "Are you ready for the big day?"

"I'm so nervous. Don't get me wrong, I love Simon and cannot wait to spend the rest of my life with him."

"But?"

"But this is a big commitment. What if I'm not a good wife? When I think about my past relationships, I see how bad of a girlfriend I was. With Luca, I tried being the perfect woman and still got screwed over."

I smiled at her. "Those fears are normal."

"I guess, but this is his second marriage, and he's a few years older. I want him to be happy."

"I'm still learning what it means to be the best partner to Sergio. All I can say is trust your instincts, and trust your partner. You and Simon will be fine."

I thought about me and Sergio and how committed we were to working through our issues. The changes wouldn't happen overnight, but as long as we kept our communication open, we'd be okay. We were still going strong after almost a month at home. Date nights were frequent after work, even if it was a simple dinner at home. Spending time with each other was our priority.

"You always know what to say, Mick." Reyla glanced my way. "You've been the most consistent person in my life. What do you think about being my matron of Honor?"

I in took a sharp breath and stared at her. "Rey, your wedding is three weeks away."

"I know, I know. But I wanted to ask you in-person. You don't need to plan a bridal shower or wear an ugly dress. You're my best friend, Michaela. I couldn't imagine doing this without you beside me."

Heat flooded my cheeks at her words. There was no way I'd say no to being her Matron of Honor, especially since I didn't have to do anything but show up. When I got married, we weren't on the best of terms. I wondered if it would have been better if she had been there every step.

"So, what do you say?" Reyla pressed after a beat.

"I'd be honored to be your matron of Honor." I grinned at her.

We giggled at my silly response.

Once our laughter subsided, she said, "Now I'm officially ready to walk down the aisle."

SERGIO'S HAND slid up my arm to my shoulder. He played with the thin strap of my dress. His thumb grazed my skin, leaving behind a trail of goosebumps. I glanced over my shoulder at him, meeting his smoldering gaze. A half-smile formed on his lips.

"You look beautiful."

I bit my lip and faced forward. "Thank you. You look incredibly handsome."

Sergio looked so good that it was hard to stay focused tonight. His fresh hair cut, enticing cologne and gold herringbone chain was a dangerously sexy combination. He wore an ivory colored button up and navy pants to match my champagne colored dress. We'd gotten compliments on our appearance all night.

The elevator chimed, prompting us to exit the elevator. We'd just left the rehearsal dinner for Reyla and Simon's wedding. Something about celebrating their union had me in my feels. I kept thinking about our wedding day, and how far we'd come.

Sergio held my hand as we walked down the long hallway to our hotel suite.

"When are you going to Reyla's room?"

"In an hour or two. She wanted to spend a moment alone before the slumber party."

He nodded. "I can work with that."

"What are you up to?" I asked with a smirk.

Pulling out the key to our room, Sergio simpered. "You'll see."

He opened the door and stepped aside for me to enter first. I gasped at the balloons, flowers, and gifts in our suite. Sergio's hands were on my waist as he guided me into the room.

"I know we're here for a wedding, but it's still Valentine's Day," he noted in my ear. "I had to show out this year."

I giggled. "You always out do yourself."

On the coffee table was a bottle of champagne, chocolate covered strawberries and two boxes. Sergio popped open the bubbly, then filled our glasses.

"Happy Valentine's Day, my love," he said while handing me my first gift. From its rectangular shape, I assumed it was a necklace. After opening the box, I knew I was right. The petite diamond tennis bracelet was beautiful. I lifted my hair so Sergio could put around my neck. It went perfectly with the necklace he'd given me as a graduation gift a few years back.

"It's beautiful. Thank you," I said before kissing him. After wiping away my lipstick from his mouth, I leaned in for one more peck.

He reached for the second box. "In a few weeks, I'll be leaving for New York. I wanted to leave you with something special."

My eyes widened at the eternity diamond ring inside.

"This is a promise ring," he explained. Removing the ring from the box, he slid it onto my right ring finger. "I promise to make time for you and to always love you. If I had to do all over again, I'd choose you. No question."

"I'll always choose you, Sergio. And I promise to love you until the end of time."

The prolonged anticipation of feeling his lips against mine was unbearable. I grabbed him by the face and kissed him hard, deep. My body hummed for his touch. I pressed into him, needing to be as close to him as possible. He grabbed me by the ass and moaned. I smiled against his lips while slipping a hand between us. I worked fast to unzip his pants.

At the feeling of his erection, I dropped to my knees and took him into my mouth. Sergio watched from above with low, enticing eyes. I sucked and slurped until his knees buckled. Using both hands, I stroked him while kissing the head. Burning sighs fell from his lips, but his gaze never left mine. Watching him unravel was truly a sight. He closed his eyes, tilted his head back, and released a low, throaty hiss. I continued going after his climax, loving the contorted expression on his handsome face. After a moment, he grabbed a handful of my hair and pulled his length from my mouth.

"What are you trying to do to me, baby?"

I stared at him with an impish smirk. "Oh, nothing. Just showing my undying appreciation for you."

He pushed out a throaty groan and helped me to my feet.

"Come here," he growled, bending me over the arm of the couch.

Hiking my dress over my hips, Sergio pushed my panties aside and spread my thighs open. He placed soft kisses on the back of my thighs and ass. I arched my back for him, giving him better access to my pussy. His tongue lashed against my clit incessantly. I held onto the chair for support, but it was no use. My knees trembled and my heart beat erratically. He didn't stop until I was a soaking mess. I loved how he took his time devouring me. He was making it hard for me to leave. I turned over and fell onto the couch. The remnants of his work dripped down my thighs as I laid lifeless.

Sergio was finished. The smirk on his face while he stroked himself warmed my insides. He unbuttoned his shirt before removing it followed by the pants around his ankle. He hooked his arm around my waist, pushing me further onto the couch.

I shuddered a breath when he thrusted into me. His strokes were slow and intoxicating. Our gazes locked, and I saw the unadulterated love he felt for me in his eyes. I caressed his cheek before pulling him down to meet my lips. We kissed each other until we were breathless. His tongue slowly danced with mine. The fire between us spread to my heart as another orgasm overcame me. Sergio's climax soon followed with one long, deep stroke.

After getting a warm wash cloth, Sergio cleaned our mess, then we laid on the couch.

I held up my right hand to admire my ring. "Your Valentine's Gift is waiting for you at home. But I kind of want to tell you what it is."

Sergio chuckled. "Go ahead."

"The Red Ranger camera I saw you looking at a while back."

He propped himself up on his elbow. "Michaela. Are you serious? That camera is-"

"Hundreds of thousands of dollars? I know, but you wanted it and I couldn't not get it. Look at all you've given me. A home, access to money, a love I can't even explain. The camera doesn't put a dent in all I owe you."

Sergio kissed me. "You are something special, Michaela. Having you in my life *is* enough."

I smiled because he really didn't understand how much *he* meant to *me*.

It was then that *I vowed* to spend the rest of my life showing Sergio how special he was to me.

THE END

Thank you for taking the time to read The Matrimony! I hope you enjoyed Michaela and Sergio's HEA.

Please consider leaving a review.

Until next time,

D.

XO
AVAILABLE NOW

I closed the space between us. My eyes bounced from his lips to his eyes. The heat in is his gaze encouraged me to do what I'd been thinking about since we met. I pressed my lips against his, relishing in the sensation of his lips. When he put his hand on my cheek, I angled my head to the side, accepting his hungry tongue that played at the seams of my lips.

His kiss was sweet as honey, with a potency that rivaled his moonshine. When our kiss ended, I opened my eyes, disappointed by it being over so soon. He tilted my head back, forcing me to meet his gaze. Warmth spread in my cheeks as I pressed into him. He caressed my cheek with the pads of his thumb. My heart fluttered, and I heaved a sigh.

"I've only known you a short time, but I can't imagine my life without you, Nola."

The softness in his brown eyes reflected how deeply he felt for me. I wanted to believe it was too good to be true. But my intuition told me this was real. The instant connection and inexplicable fondness between us showed me this was real. From the moment we met, our chemistry had been explosive. I wanted to relish in it for as long as I could.

"I'm not going anywhere because, oddly enough, I don't want to imagine life without you, either."

He kissed me again. This time, he took his time nipping and pecking at my lips.

ACKNOWLEDGMENTS

God, for this gift!
CCJ, for your wisdom, accountability, and support throughout this entire writing process
Eddie, for supporting me through my long days and nights of writing, revising, & editing!
Family and friends, for you alls unwavering support <3

ALSO BY D. ROSE

Standalone Titles:

Cherie Amour

Yearning for Your Love

True Love for Christmas

Milk & Honey: a collection of shorts

Love's Language

Warmth

Share My World

Pieces of Love

Love on Repeat

My One Christmas Wish

A New Year With You

The Vow*

Together Again

The New Year Resolution

Songs in the Key of Love

Remedy

Series Titles:

Fire & Desire:

Love Me Up

Take You Down

For Keeps:

New Year Kiss (A Short Story)

Because of Love

The Sweetest Love

On Love's Time

Hidden Lake Series:

Alone With You (#2)

Roseville:

Brown Sugar

Ready for Love

Second Chance:

Another Chance to Love

All I Need is You

The Boos and Booze Series:

Brewing Storm (#6)

The Luminous Cruise Chronicles:

Love Overboard (#3)

CURRENT: An Anthology For Jackson

Made in the USA
Columbia, SC
18 May 2025